The Moon Bunny & the Sun Lion

AN ARCANA GLEN SWEET PARANORMAL ROMANCE

TAROT ELF FANTASY MAJOR ARCANA SERIES
BOOK NINE

TARA MAYA

Misque Press

An Arcana Glen Sweet Paranormal Romance

The Major Arcana Series, Book 9

"The Moon Bunny & the Sun Lion"

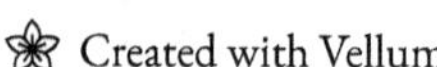 Created with Vellum

Welcome to Arcana Glen, a magical town hidden in the Rocky Mountains of Colorado....

Here arcanes of all types are free to be themselves... Elves, Witches, Shifters, Seraphs, Dragons and more.

But until the Twenty-Two Guardians are restored to power, the Elven War rages among the arcanes. What's the solution?

True Love, of course!

To read a free love story and sneak a peek at what happened before the Massacre of the Guardians, ten years ago, CLICK HERE to sign up for the newsletter for Tara's Tribe and receive the free novella, *The Genie & the Gymnast.*

The Genie & the Gymnast

FREE NOVELLA

THE GENIE

Jay Zee is a Jinn. He knows better than to grant wishes to humans. But he makes an exception in exchange for a shot at his dream job: working for the Magician. He never expects the old man to demand that Jay Zee marry his daughter...or that she is the most hideously ugly woman on Earth. As a terrible danger closes in on all of them, Jay Zee starts to question what is most important ... but it may be too late to stop a massacre.

THE GYMNAST

To her friends in the Enchanted Circus, Janet seems like a pretty, young, carefree performer. Even among other arcanes, she has to keep the secret of her true nature. Janet can't believe that her father forced her into marriage with a Jinn. She knows her new husband loathes her, but she can't help but dream that he might look past her twisted exterior.

This tale is a stand-alone HEA love story set ten years before most of the stories from Arcana Glen, on the eve of the Massacre of the Guardians.

Click here to join Tara's Tribe of Readers to and receive the latest news on more romantic fantasy stories and read The Genie and the Gymnast.

Email: editor@misquepress.com to request a free Review Copy of any of Tara Maya's novels.

Dahlia was hired to hunt down a Lion Shifter who stole a deadly weapon.

Aaresh was a mild-mannered school teacher by day. By night, he turned into a monster he couldn't control...

But when Dahlia hunts him down and he traps her in his lair, who is the hunter and who is the prey?

Welcome to Arcana Glen, a magical town hidden in the Rocky Mountains of Colorado....
Here arcanes of all types are free to be themselves... Elves, Witches, Shifters, Seraphs, Dragons and more.

One

September 5
Sunrise: 06:40
Sunset: 19:30
Moon: Waxing gibbous
Daylight: 12:49 hours

IT'S PERFECTLY *normal to be nervous on your first day of school*, Aaresh Raj reminded himself. He packed his books, a fresh notebook, a three-ring binder, a case full of nice pens and freshly sharpened number two pencils.

Especially if you have been homeschooled all your life, he thought. He wiped his sweaty hands on his pants and picked up his books. He walked toward the campus from the parking lot. *Especially if this is your first day going to a regular school with regular students.*

His heart was pounding in his chest. It's normal to be nervous on your first day of school, especially if the tutors that you learned from as a child were also scientists who experimented on you with no regard for your civil liberties or human rights.

He found the door to the classroom open and entered. It was difficult because he was quite large.

Especially if you have body size problems, he thought grimly.

He looked at the desks. Although it was a "normal" school to him, Arcana Glen Academy wasn't a public school but a private institution that catered to magic users. There were only 12 desks in the classroom arranged in a semi-circle around a huge desk in front of a whiteboard.

The desks were so clean they gleamed like mirrors. Then he realized they *were* mirrors—magic mirrors. Strange —but it *was* a school for magic.

He glanced down at the shiny surface of a student desk. Oh dear. He could see his mane and his muzzle clearly. It was not a human face, but the face of a huge golden lion.

Especially if you're stuck in the form of a big, giant animal.

Finally, he went to go sit at *his* desk. The big one.

Especially if you're the teacher.

The glamour didn't work! Aaresh quietly panicked, staring at his own reflection in his mirror-surface desk. He contemplated escape. He was ready to leap up and race from the classroom, but at that moment, the principal of the school trotted in.

Ms Mercado was a centaur, and because the school was closed to mundane outsiders, she wasn't shy about wearing her arcane form, the lower portion of a horse and the upper portion of a woman in a silk shirt and blazer and scarf. Her hair was done up on her head. She was almost 1000 years old, and it showed as the age lines of a middle-aged human woman in her face.

"Good," she said briskly. "There you are Mr Raj. You arrived early. I wanted to make certain you were settled."

"The glamour didn't work," he exclaimed. "I just saw my reflection and I clearly still look like a lion!"

"Naturally, *you* are able to see your own reflection," said Ms Mercado. "This particular glamour is not designed work on *you*, the person in disguise. But I assure you, to everyone else you look as if you are a Centaur, just like me. No one can tell you are a Lion. Although I really don't know why you insist on hiding it. Most shape shifters would love to be able to speak as perfect English as you do in their animal form."

Aaresh Raj cleared his throat. "It's important to me. It's part of the contract I signed."

"Yes, and we will certainly honor it. I just don't think it's necessary, but it's your choice. Your credentials were very impressive across-the-board and we are excited to have you here at Arcana Academy, the perfect school for illuminating magic minds."

She said it as though she were reading aloud from the school's brochure.

"There are a few things I'd like to go over with you," the Centaur Principal continued. "One, you will have your students come to you. You will teach three different classes. We only hold academic classes in the morning. Magic is taught in the afternoon. Are you sure you don't wish to teach magic...?"

"I prefer to teach human subjects," he said firmly.

"We are looking for a volunteer to help with the choir.

Would you be interested in it? I noticed on your résumé you said that you played several instruments."

She cocked her head at him as if trying to imagine how he played the violin and the piano with his immense paws. Honestly, it was all in the claws. But what would that look like in the glamour of a Centaur? Would he look like he was playing with his human hands, or with his hooves?

"I will definitely consider it," he promised.

"There's one other little item," she said. "We know that territory is very important to many Shifters. Especially..." She cleared her throat delicately. "Top predators. However, you will have to share your classroom."

A growl began deep in his throat against his will. Aaresh cut off the embarrassing animal response immediately.

She had noticed, however. She stepped back just a tiny fraction of a step. The glamour might work on other people, but the principal knew very well that he was a lion as large as an African elephant. Fortunately, the classrooms were designed for magical creatures, and were large enough to even accommodate dragons. Otherwise, he would not have been able to fit his body through the door.

"It's necessary because the school has found it expedient to rent out these classrooms in the evening to adult night school programs," explained Principal Mercado. "It helps us keep our fees low so that we can take poor but magically gifted students. However, it means that there will be a teacher in your classroom during the evenings, from 6 to 10 pm. She will not be here during the day, and you will probably not cross paths with her if you leave here by 5 o'clock, as your contract mandates. Nor is she allowed to be on the campus during our regular hours. You should never run into each other.

"However," Ms Mercado added, "I understand your

sense of smell is very sensitive and you will probably pick up her scent. I'm explaining that you don't need to worry about it, it is legitimate. You will get used to it in time. Please keep the classroom neat and don't leave any of your belongings here overnight.

"Good luck on your first day."

The bell rang and the children began to file in. Because it was a small school, there was a spread of ages. His first class was the youngest. He suspected right away they would be his favorite. They were the 6th and 7th graders. When they pointed to him and called him Mr Horsey-Butt, he knew that the principal was right, his glamour was in place.

The illusion was very sophisticated. Unlike illusions aimed at deceiving humans, this one had to fool other Shifters and Witches as well. If therefore covered all the senses, not just what he looked like, but the sounds he made, the scents he emitted. The soft pitter-pat of his paws would sound to others like the hard clippity-clap of hooves on the pavement; the noises from his throat that were really growls would sound to the children like the knicker of a horse. The feel of his fur would be not quite as soft as his real fur, but a little rougher like the flank of a stallion. And most importantly of all, his smell would be masked. To any Shifter, he would not smell like a predator, but like prey.

It was strange that he felt safer disguised as a prey animal then as the so-called King of the Jungle. But he had learned the hard way that being at the top of the food chain meant nothing when dealing with human beings. There was always another predator stronger than you, and the stronger you looked to humans, the more determined they were to take you down. Because of his size he couldn't disguise himself as something truly innocent and harmless. Pretending to be a Mouse Shifter would have been nice, he thought wistfully, but that would strain the glamour too far.

Still, he was happy with his false identity. No one was terrified of a Centaur.

The second class was a little older than the first class and much rowdier. They were 8th, 9th and 10th graders, and completely in the grips of their hormones.

But it was the third class, the cynical, older High Schoolers, that Aaresh found the most difficult to relate to. The boys and girls of his Juniors and Seniors class were also much more interested in impressing each other than impressing him. But they were cleverer about their games of one-upmanship, and, as he feared, they used defiance of the teacher as a way to show off to each other about their sophistication and independence.

They talked constantly while he tried to explain the curriculum to them. Unlike the middle school kids, who are simply bouncing off the walls from an excess of energy like over-wound wind-up toys, the High School students lounged in their chairs, chewed gum, munched snacks, put on make-up and played games on their phones. He wasn't able to force them to pay attention to him.

He had no idea how to keep discipline, he realized. When he had been a student, his situation had been one small child with several teachers at a time, rather than one teacher faced with twelve students. (How on earth did public school teachers with a class of 30 or more cope with it?!)

Additionally, had Aaresh ever dared act out of line, the teacher-scientist had the right to literally administer a jolt through electrode implants in his dermis and cause a shock like electric shock therapy in an insane asylum. Aaresh would never have *dared* to defy his teachers, never mind speak while one was speaking.

After the last bell rang, Aaresh felt wrung out and exhausted. Only one day had passed and he already felt like a failure. Why had he thought he could do any normal job like a normal person or even a normal shifter?

He had never been normal. He'd never had a normal family. He's never gone to a normal school. He was nothing but a mutant freak created in a laboratory.

And if the principal ever found out the truth about him, his dirtiest secret, he would definitely be fired. Even if his secret never came out, at this rate, Aaresh feared losing his job simply for being a terrible teacher.

Or he might really screw up and accidentally eat a student.

His one respite had been in the middle of the day. At lunch time, he availed himself of the cafeteria, piling up his tray with three plates of food: one plate with roasted beef, fried chicken, hot dogs and bacon. The second plate held nothing but a heap of scrambled eggs. The third plate was filled with sweets: a slice of chocolate cake, strawberry jello, and fruit embedded in marshmallow.

He took his tray into the teacher's lounge, which was a quarter the size of the student's cafeteria. He sat alone at a table, away from the other teachers who sat in clumps. He wasn't used to eating in a social setting. In the laboratory, the shifters were fed alone in the cells.

To his surprise, a Dwarf strode to his table and thrust

out his hand. "Erik Orecoat. I teach Math, Engineering and Elementary Elemental Stone magic. You must be the new English teacher."

Aaresh held out his hand and shook hands with Erik. "Aaresh Raj."

Erik sat down and ate lunch with him, sustaining a friendly, if shallow, conversation. Erik also introduced Aaresh to the other teachers. None of them questioned his cover story. Aaresh had dreaded meeting his fellow teachers, sure that they would see through him as a fake, but it wasn't as bad as he'd feared at all.

Aaresh packed up all his books and notebooks and pens and pencils at the end of the day. He put them in the satchel with his paws and carried the satchel handle in his mouth. He carried it out to the parking lot, and then he kept going. He didn't have a car. He pretended that he walked home, but the truth was he lived in the forest. When he escaped, he had taken with him the knowledge of several patents and inventions. They were all his own ideas, although technically he was not the owner of them. Unable to truly profit from them, he had sold them secretly on the black market to the enemies of the company that owned the patents.

Not very nice. Not very legal. But what they had done to him was not nice or legal either. He received the cash, converted it from digital currency to gold, and used the fund to buy a house as well as create a little nest egg for himself.

He didn't need to teach for a living. But the alternative was to live in isolation like a hermit. He couldn't bear to do that. He was afraid of people, but he *needed* people. He wanted them to love him and appreciate him. He wanted to be worthy of that love and appreciation. The one thing he had acquired in growing up in a laboratory as a test subject was a broad knowledge of dozens of topics. It always amused his captors to watch him struggle to perform human actions in his lion form.

Not all of his tutors had been brutes. Some of them had been the closest Aaresh ever had to caring parental figures. Maybe that was why despite everything he'd been through, and the trauma associated with it, he still loved learning and hoped to pass that love on to his own students.

It's only the first day, he reminded himself. It's too soon to give up. You'll do better tomorrow. It's natural to be nervous on your first day of school.

Two

September 6
Sunrise: 06:41
Sunset: 19:27
Moon: Waxing gibbous
Daylight: 12:47 hours

DAHLIA MOON EXAMINED the classroom where she would be teaching. It could have been worse. At least there were no crayon drawings or blocks with the ABCs on them. Still, she doubted her adult students, who were there to study how to become licensed bounty hunters for arcane cases in the state of Colorado, were going to appreciate the posters on adverbs or quotes from *Twelfth Night* ("Some are born great, some achieve greatness, and some have greatness thrust upon them.") It was a High School classroom and the decor reflected that.

But the bigger problem was the desks and chairs. They were all attached to each other, which meant they were not suited for a muscular male adult 6 foot tall, which would be most of her students. She spent a few moments unlatching the desks and spreading them further apart.

At least they weren't kindergartener desks, like last semester. Dahlia had been the only one who could fit in the chairs.

Dahlia was a "Bunny Shifter,"—properly called a Yuetu, a Rabbit Shifter–cute and fluffy in her alter form and diminutive in her human form as well, at 4"8" and 92 pounds. It was the main reason that she was *teaching* bounty hunting rather than doing it. Getting jobs in the arcane world usually was more than just a matter of getting a bail bond to hire you. Usually, you had to have a personal interview with the arcane who wanted someone found in the Mundane Sphere. You had to have a human license as well, so you needed a cover story, and legal right to apprehend someone.

But some arcanes involved wanted more than that. They wanted to know you had the magic and the power, the kick and the punch, to get the job done. And most of the arcane world regarded Bunny Shifters as adorable, sweet, kind, harmless and if useful for anything, good at cooking and serving snacks.

Most of her family were perfect examples of the stereotype. Her mother and father ran a little pastry shop and restaurant called *Bao & Bun*. They thought Dalia was crazy for trying to become a bounty hunter.

The students started filing in. They looked at her and she could see the incredulity in their eyes. They didn't care about the posters about adverbs or *Twelfth Night*, they cared that the teacher didn't look like someone they could respect.

Dahlia was used to it and stared them down. Usually

prey shifters like her couldn't meet the eyes of top predators like the Wolf Shifter who was the first man to walk in through the door. He was over 6 feet and had a bicycle-lock chain wrapped around one arm. He looked more like he should be wanted by bounty hunters than becoming one.

He grinned at her and immediately invaded her space. "Did you come to the wrong classroom, honey bunny?"

Of course, as a Shifter, he knew she was a rabbit as soon as she knew he was a wolf. You couldn't hide your scent from Shifters.

Dahlia stood on the balls of her feet, tense and ready in case he tried to touch her. She had a very simple rule. No touching.

He poked one finger at her chest. Maybe he thought he was flirting. Dahlia was not amused. She shifted into rabbit form, darted between his legs, shifted back to human, grabbing his arm on the way back up to her full height. Coming at him from behind where he didn't expect it, she was able to twist his arm in such a way that his body was forced to follow the movement and he flipped over onto his back.

He wheezed at her, stunned.

"You're Zachery Gnawfang, correct?" Dahlia asked.

His eyes bugged; Dahlia could tell he was wondering if she also had psychic magic. In fact, she did, but only Empathy, which wouldn't have told her his name. She'd merely made an educated guess based on the roster.

She said calmly, "My name is Dalia Moon. You may call me Ms Moon. I am your instructor. Never touch me. Sit in your seat and pay attention if you want to pass this class."

He rubbed his neck and almost whimpered as he found a seat.

Every time she taught this class, she had to make some sort of demonstration like that to prove she was worthy of respect. But the good thing about Shifters was that only one demonstration was necessary. Once other students filed into the class, even though no one else had witnessed what she had done, they also noted the tall, strong wolf Shifter sitting respectfully, watching her with an air of submission.

They all looked from her to him and back to her again, puzzled and finally intimidated. Sometimes stereotypes worked in her favor.

They looked at her and saw a diminutive attractive woman with two black ponytails and the features of a Korean American, and probably subconsciously or consciously comparing her to the Dragon Empress. The Dragon Empress was the most powerful shifter in Arcana Glen, and she also looked like a delicate china doll. Dahlia could see them moving her from the category of "harmless bunny" to "deadly ninja princess."

She wasn't a ninja, and she wasn't a princess, but she liked to think that she could be deadly if she needed to. She had never killed anyone. She was a bounty hunter, not an assassin.

A bounty hunter and a teacher. She picked up a marker and started writing on the whiteboard.

"This is our course of study. Bail recovery, 16 hours. Principles of criminal culpability, three hours, Colorado criminal code, three hours. Arcane criminal code, five hours. Firearms and weapons, two hours. Spells and magical attacks, three hours. Illusions and glamours, two hours..." And so, through all the subjects she intended to cover down to bail bond industry ethics.

As she lectured, keeping her voice steady and even and her presentation factual rather than entertaining, she studied the students sitting in the seats. Almost all twelve seats were filled. There was only one student on her roster missing. Yuri something or other.

All the other names were accounted for during rollcall. As usual it was mostly Shifters or Demi-shifters. And even among shifters, there were divisions. The White Wolves who served the Winter Elves were hated by all the other Wolf Shifters, as well as by Werewolves. Fortunately, there were none of those in her class, just two Wolf Shifters from different packs who kept glaring at each other. Sooner or later, they would fight for dominance, in their wolf form, but stop short of killing one another. (She hoped.) Once dominance order was established, they'd probably get along fine.

There was also a Bear Shifter, steady and unflappable, pretty typical for his kind. There was a Weasel Shifter. He had eaten fish right before he came to class and the smell bothered Dahlia. There were also two men that had no animal scent, whom she took to be humans who were either Witches or sensitive to magic. Both of them were male, and she wasn't sure if they preferred to be called witches, warlocks, or wizards. Human magic users got offended if you called them the "wrong" title, but they themselves couldn't agree on such matters. Humans were more diffi-cult to deal with than Shifters.

There was one very interesting student whom Dahlia couldn't quite pigeon-hole. The woman was the only female in the class, but that wasn't what intrigued Dahlia. To mundane humans, humans who were completely insen-sitive to any form of magic, to the point that they often couldn't see it even if it happened right in front of them, the woman would look like she had a stump cut off at her right shoulder. The US Air Force T-shirt she wore hinted that the injury might have been combat related.

But to arcane eyes, she had a huge crab claw, like the oversized right claw on a fiddler club except sized for a humanoid. It looked deadly and intimidating as hell. At least the woman was unlikely to experience the usual hazing of a female student in a male dominated field. The claw spoke for itself.

Dahlia had never heard of any kind of Crab Shifter. She longed to hear the story behind that appendage, but it was probably a sensitive subject. A curse might even be involved.

Sometimes Dahlia established friendships with students, and they opened up by the end of the twelve-week class together. Sometimes it didn't happen. She wouldn't force it. During class itself, she always stuck to business.

Dahlia had just started going over distinction between human law and arcane law and why they had to follow both as long as they were on Earth, when a late pair of students arrived.

She had only been expecting one extra student. One of them she recognized—and he was not on her roster— Logan Barq.

Logan Barq was a White Wolf, and he didn't hide it. He had the same coloring as many Shifters and Elves from Winterdom: platinum-white hair (in his case, buzzed short), snow-pale skin and glacier blue eyes. But even if that didn't give him away, he had a silver brand on his right bicep that marked him as a "Squire," a euphemism for the special chattel of an Azir Lord. If Logan had bothered to wear a sleeved shirt, the metallic brand wouldn't have shown, but today he wore a sleeveless t-shirt and jeans, as if he simply gave zero fudgesicles what anyone thought. Only someone, like Dahlia, who had memorized all the sigils of the noble Elf families of Winterdom would realize that the magic in Logan's brand had been destroyed by an angry slash across the whole thing. To a casual observer, the extra mark probably looked like part of the complex design.

Dahlia met Logan's eyes, which were glowing silver, a sign he was on high alert. She wanted to ask him about the upcoming contest, but it wouldn't be professional to discuss it in the classroom. But if he wasn't here to discuss their upcoming partnership, why was Logan here?

Every Wolf Shifter in the room, not to mention the Bear and Claw Lady, looked at the White Wolf Shifter with hostility. Earth was neutral in the war that was raging between the Elven realms, but every arcane had relatives who had suffered at the hands of the Winter Elves and their servants and allies such as the White Wolves.

"Logan is a Ranger. He works on a security team for the Guardians," Dahlia announced to no one in particular. Logan reported to Prince Delson, a Summer Elf, not a Winter Elf. Prince Delson was the brother of the Guardian known as the Emperor. Those in the class who had been growling at the back of their throats stopped immediately.

Logan cast her a wry look as if to say, *I don't need your charity.* Dahlia raised her eyebrows. *I'm not doing it for you,* her look retorted. And she wasn't. She didn't need the trouble the misunderstanding would bring. It was best just to clear the air right away. Everyone here was on the same side.

That couldn't be said of everyone who lived in Arcana Glen. Unfortunately, there *was* an entire nest of Winter Elves and their minions, including clueless humans who thought they were in charge, over at a base under a mountain northwest of the town. They kept to themselves, which was just as well. They were not welcome in polite society.

"I brought your final student." Logan gestured to the man behind him, a big guy with tattoos all over his body, and a shaved head—and fangs.

Automatically, Dahlia sniffed to find out what kind of Shifter he was. Her nostrils flared at the whiff of death. He was no animal.

The other students also smelled the vile odor.

"That's a freaking Vampire!" Zachery Gnawfang spat in disgust.

If there was one thing that could unite Shifters of any kind, it was their mutual hatred for Vampires.

"Are you kidding me?" Dahlia asked Logan.

"He's newly turned," said Logan, "And he's never killed anyone. He's been staying like a good little Vampire up at the Magician's Castle as our special... guest."

Dahlia snorted. She had never been to the Castle, but she had heard rumors that there were dungeons underneath that could hold anything, even a Dragon. She had a feeling the Vampire, 'guest' or not, had been staying in *that* part of the castle.

"Now he's been given a chance to show that he can be a responsible citizen," Logan went on. "So he needs to get some job training."

"I already *had* job," growled the Vampire.

"Valet/hitman is not a respectable position. This is better. Trust me, you'll like it. Just give it a chance."

"Are you going to stay with him?" asked Dahlia.

Logan sighed. "I have no choice. The Vampire is still on probation. If he proves he can control himself..." Logan shrugged. "I don't know how long that will take. Probably longer than your course. If he takes your class, I have to take it."

"And dis is job you vant me to take? Taught by *Bunny Shifter*?" asked the Vampire. "It sucks." He glanced around the high school classroom. "Vhat in hell does Shakespearrr have to do vith bounty hunting?"

At least someone besides her had noticed the posters.

Three

CLASS ENDED around four hours after sunset, at 23:00. Dahlia wanted to talk to Logan about his plans for the Autumn Twilight Festival. She wanted to remind him that it was going to come up early this year and also remind him of his promise that he would help her with the challenge. But she felt curiously shy to talk to him in front of the Vampire. Obviously, the Guardians weren't yet sure they could trust the undead creature.

She postponed the conversation for now and simply said goodbye. Logan offered her a ride home, but she turned him down. She liked to jog, and she was something of a night owl. Which was a little odd considering she was a Bunny Shifter. Just another way she was unusual.

It was almost a 45-minute jog home. The moon was Waxing Gibbous on this fine September night. Arcana Glen was high enough up in the mountains that it was already quite nippy. Like most Shifters, Dahlia didn't mind the cold. It hadn't snowed yet, but it was growing bitterly cold. If it rained tonight, there would be snow.

She was aware that predators came out at night, and that if they saw her and knew her for a Bunny Shifter, they would consider giving chase. That was another reason she liked to run at night. Sometimes she drew bad guys out of the woodwork, and if they attacked, she was morally free to fight back. If she took a few thugs and rapists out of the population by serving as bait, it was a service she was happy to render to the community of arcanes.

Sometimes being constantly underestimated sucked. But sometimes it was freaking fantastic. The key to winning any battle was to work with your strength and your opponent's weaknesses, and never, *ever* be *where* they expected or *what* they expected. Nobody expected a Bunny Shifter to be a huntress. That's why it worked so well for her.

The loneliest portion of her run home was through a thick pine forest. When Dahlia entered the tree cover, she heard another runner's footsteps pacing behind her to match her foot falls. Someone was following her. He was using stealth, trying to hide his presence. Almost certainly he was up to nothing good.

It was going to be one of those nights when some cocky, predacious Shifter attacked Dahlia to rob her, rape her, kidnap her or kill her.

Awesome.

She looked forward to taking out another loser who thought to prey on the weak.

Adrenaline zinged through her body, followed by the zip-zap tingling feeling of magic growing and pooling in her fingertips.

There was nothing special about the magical talent she had been born with. Like all Rabbit Shifters, her ancestors originally came from Springvale. Elemental Water magic came easily to her. In terms of her psychic abilities, she did not have telepathy, but again like many Springvale arcanes, she had some Empathy.

Water Magic and Empathy: that was all. Like being a Bunny shifter, that combination of powers suggested to most people that Dahlia should have chosen a career in something soft and comforting, like healer, counselor, gardener or cook.

Ha. Not Dahlia.

She had honed her generic magic to be focused and specific. She enhanced her natural ability to run and hide to become *completely invisible* through a glamour that used mist and refractions to camouflage herself in any environment. If there wasn't enough Elemental Water in the dry Colorado atmosphere, she drew on one of the leylines under Arcana Glen, veins of magic that had been laid by mages like an energy grid under the whole area. These rivers or tendrils of magic were not native to this earthly sphere. They stretched out from any spot where magic from the other spheres was frequently used. Magic users called them leylines and tried to live near them so that they could tap into the magic the way the appliances in a house would tap into the electrical grid.

She could also create a rope out of Elemental Water that she could climb high into the sky, which she could use to evade any predator. She called that her *Climb to the Moon* trick.

And she had honed her sense of Empathy to detect any predator in her vicinity.

These two common abilities, through hard work, diligence, study, and practice, she had turned into three very specific and unique skills. Her techniques were all the more powerful because no one had any way to anticipate that she had those talents merely from looking at her or smelling her or knowing her kind. They were unique to her, to Dahlia Moon.

She extended her Empathy into the area around her, feeling for the predatory mind. She was puzzled. She did not encounter any hunting sentience. And yet she had the sense of being hunted. She trusted her instinct.

She adjusted her pace, noting that the one who was shadowing her also adjusted his pace. Her hearing was excellent, and she was certain her stalker was a man, either human or humanoid—at the moment—probably a good hundred pounds heavier than she was, but obviously athletic, deliberately slowing his pace and shortening his stride to match hers.

And yet she couldn't sense his mind hunting her.

She couldn't smell any animal either. The wind was going the wrong direction to let her sniff him, but if he was something dangerous, she should have at least been able to pick up the odor of a Wolf or a Hell Hound or a Dragon. To a Rabbit Shifter, even a Weasel or an Owl stank like a predator.

Whoever was chasing her could have special abilities as well. Special abilities that were like hers, indistinguishable from ordinary powers unless one knew how they had been trained and honed.

Either that, or the person following her was genuinely *not* hunting her.

She slowed down and the man following her also slowed down. She picked up her pace and he picked up his pace.

She came to a complete stop. "Who are you?" she shouted. "Why are you following me?"

The footsteps stopped.

And then, a moment later, a man swung down out of a tree, spun himself in the air like a martial artist, and landed only a few feet from her. He was gorgeous, gleaming with sweat, his hair wild and dark and uncombed.

And he was stark naked.

His eyes burned with the intensity of a pure predator.

Once he captured her gaze with his, her breath caught in her throat and she went completely still. Her whole body responded to his presence. It wasn't fear that made her flush and freeze at the same time, but a visceral feminine response to a masculine paragon. He stared at her as if she were the one who was naked. And he wanted her.

He had to be arcane, but she couldn't tell what kind. In human form, he was huge, like a Greek statue, a study in chiseled muscles, a paragon brought to life. His skin was golden teak, gleaming almost like polished brass even in the cool moonlight. He had a huge shaggy mane of jet-black hair and a chin rough with a roguish buzz of a beard. But his eyes showed no iota of mercy. He was wild, human but utterly feral.

He stepped toward her. His intentions were as naked as his body, as obvious as his arousal. He intended to take her.

And as he drew closer, step by step, Dahlia couldn't... no, not couldn't, but didn't... move. Her body undulated in a show of subconscious surrender, welcoming him...

Victory curled his lips into a grin.

Her mind rebelled. She would *not* be conquered by this naked Wild Man. Although her instincts urged her to lie down and show him her... belly, she refused to give in to the urge. He would find she was not easy prey after all. But she couldn't shift. Her inner Bunny wanted him in human form. Bunny knew exactly what the Wild Man wanted and she wanted to give it to him.

He reached her, threw her to the ground, and pinned her down under him, with her wrists over her head. It was a sexually submissive position, somethings she was painfully aware of because he was butt naked and—her inner Bunny observed gleefully—*'armed with a mighty staff.'* Dahlia tried to shift to her alter form again, but her inner Bunny refused to cooperate. Damn her—the nymphomaniac bunny thought this was *fun*. Bunny flooded her mind with all the delicious ways that Sexy Wild Man could have his wicked way with her. Instead of drawing on Bunny for help, Dahlia had to shove the animal deep inside, so her raunchy thoughts wouldn't distract Dahlia.

Part of Dahlia's game was to act more afraid than she was and look weaker than she was. She wasn't about to admit that she was struggling inside with her bunny, so she pretended not to know why she couldn't shift. She faked a quaver in her voice when she asked, "What have you done to me? How did you stop me from shifting?"

Sometimes she could goad her opponents into boasting about their special magical techniques or super strength.

But this man with the golden skin and black hair only stared down at her with child-like wonder on his face. His expression of innocent delight was completely incompatible with his rough, masculine features and sexual leer. He was not a young boy, but a man in his prime. Yet his pleasure in subduing was that of a child who won a game.

He had gorgeous eyes, dark brown, but they suddenly flashed gold.

Like a Shifter. Like a Predator. And yet she still sensed nothing predatory in his emotions. In fact, as she probed his emotions—and he had no shield at all around his mind—she recognized that he thought he was playing with her. His mind was like that of a kitten, batting at a string. No wonder he behaved like a predator but didn't trigger her instinctual fear of being targeted as prey.

This gorgeous and physically fit and fully sexually mature man had the mind of a child. No, she realized as he stared down at her and his expression changed. Not a child. *An animal.* There was nothing *human* about this human male. His mind was adult, yet without any higher cognitive function. However, that didn't mean he wasn't sexually aware of her as a woman. He was—the same way a tom cat would be aware of a female cat in heat.

And that was very dangerous.

He ripped open her shirt and bent his head to lick her breast. Teasing, sweet licks brought his mouth to her nipple, and he sucked it into his mouth. A shudder of pleasure rippled through her.

Oh, yes, hummed Bunny.

Hell, no! Dahlia corrected.

Dahlia gave up trying to shape shift and did it the old-fashioned way. She used all of her skills and all of her strength to twist and squirm around under him, even at the risk of increasing his already obvious arousal, in order to get her feet into a position that she could plant an enormous, double-legged kick against his chest.

She had strong legs. She finally managed to throw him

off of her long enough that she could start running. As she ran, she tossed her Water Rope up into the sky and swung her body up onto it. The rope disappeared below her as she climbed up so there was nothing left for him to follow, even if he had known how to climb a rope. From the bewildered expression on his face that she saw when she looked down, he had never seen a rope before, never mind a magic rope.

It dawned on him that he was losing her. He began to howl like a dog at the moon.

Dahlia kept climbing into the sky until she was far enough above him that all he could do was pace below her and howl.

Unfortunately, she couldn't move her rope in any other direction. It only went straight up. She had to wait until he lost interest and left.

It took hours. But finally, toward the dawn, he gave up howling and pacing and trying to reach up to grab her. He jogged away, back into the forest.

Exhausted and a little humbled by how close she had come to something very bad, Dahlia finally let her rope down. She was cautious in case he had been only withdrawing to trick her. Somehow, with his simple mind, she doubted that. Nonetheless she didn't feel completely safe until she ran all the way home.

And here she had been so proud of her little bag of tricks. She had to remember that it was a big universe, and she wasn't the only one with secrets.

Four

September 7
Sunrise: 06:42
Sunset: 19:27
Moon: Waxing gibbous
Daylight: 12:44 hours

DAHLIA WAS EXHAUSTED. She kept late hours but that didn't mean she could go without sleep. In fact, she planned to sleep all day. She would set her alarm just to make certain she woke up in time for her class. No, wait, it was Wednesday; she didn't need to worry about her class; she only taught two nights a week, Tuesday and Thursday.

Perfect. No alarm. She would sleep until the moon came out again.

"I can't believe you're still asleep." Someone rocked Dahlia back-and-forth. Then shouted, not to her, but to someone downstairs, "MA! I found her!"

Dahlia opened her eyes and shut them again. Her sister Lily was trying to wake her up.

"What are you doing, haven't you forgotten that we are driving over to grandma's house today to cook?"

"Cook?"

Dahlia said this as if she had never heard of this strange activity.

"The festival is early this year, have you forgotten?"

The Autumn Twilight Festival! Dahlia sat up, panicked. How long had she slept?

"Is it already September 10?"

"No," said her sister. "Thank goodness, since we haven't made anything yet. We have to start cooking. We're not only making the food for our family, but we need to have extra for the booth. If you would ever come and work a shift in the restaurant you would know that."

Dahlia worked shifts in the restaurant all the time, far too often, considering it wasn't her job, she didn't get paid, and she didn't even want to do it. Just because everyone else in her family wanted to cook pastries for a living didn't mean she had to do so too. She glanced at the clock and when she saw the date and time, she groaned.

"Go away, I'm going to sleep for another two hours."

"Two hours!"

"It's only 8 o'clock in the morning," pointed out Dahlia. "And I didn't get in this morning until 5:20."

"Did a guy keep you busy?" Her sister smirked.

"As a matter of fact, yes. He was like an animal, he wouldn't rest, he just kept going and going."

Her sister rolled her eyes. "You want me to think you're

making a sexual innuendo, but I can already tell you're just talking about one of your boring bounty hunts."

Dahlia shrugged. Then she yawned. "One more hour…"

"No, we have to go now. I'll help you get dressed. Go take a shower. You *look* like you spent all night with a guy, and grandma will be scandalized."

"The woman who outlived five human husbands doesn't have anything to be scandalized about."

"She likes men. But she did marry each of them first."

Unlike many arcanes, Rabbit Shifters were unusually eager and willing to find mates among mundanes. The ability to change shape only had a 50-50 chance of being passed down to the next generation, and then it became increasingly unlikely that descendants would share the ability. But since shifting into a rabbit wasn't considered a huge asset in the first place, no one cared. Or maybe it was just the nature of the Yuetu to be very affectionate. They fell in love easily, and also, not surprisingly, they were very fertile. Some shifters had a harder time producing offspring if they married a human, but not Rabbit Shifters. They had oodles of babies.

It also meant that a one-night stand without physical and magical protection risked a disaster. One time was *definitely* all it would take to knock up any female Rabbit Shifter.

"I don't have any dates," said Dahlia. "I don't know why."

Her sister looked at her incredulously. "Maybe it's due to your compulsion to knock a guy on his ass the minute you meet him. Next time you meet a tall, gorgeous hunk, resist the urge to punch him in the face."

"I only do that in my bounty hunting classes and I actually have a reason."

"Really? Because it seems to me your reason is that the more attracted you are to a guy, the more you have to try to push him away. And the better looking he is, the more compelled you are to try to prove you're some kind of bad ass warrior instead of just flirting with him like a normal Bunny."

Dahlia decided this was a pointless conversation and put her pillow over her head.

"Come on!" Her sister dragged her out of bed and shoved Dahlia towards the bathroom. "Go shower. You stink. You smell like were trapped in the forest up a a tree all night."

"Something like that," muttered Dahlia.

"You know it's cats that are supposed to climb trees, not rabbits?"

Dahlia did feel better after taking a shower. She thought her sister would be gone when she came back out, but no, Lily was still there sorting through clothes.

"I figured I might as well help you pick out your outfit for the festival because you probably haven't done that either," Lily explained as she laid out several sundresses with accouterments.

"I have, actually. And it's none of those things."

Dahlia showed her the outfit she had picked out.

"That looks like something Laura Tomb Raider would wear," Lily scoffed.

Dahlia smiled at the khaki cargo shorts, utility belt and sturdy boots. "Yeah. Isn't it cute? What's even better is there are a lot more hidden pockets that you can't see from the outside."

"You're going there to sell moon cakes at a booth. What did we just say about not punching new people?"

"There's also going to be contests. Archery, Fireball throwing, wrestling..."

"By. The. Light. Please tell me you are not planning to... You are, aren't you! Did you get Logan to agree to help you? I'm going to tell mom. She will forbid it!

"She will try. If some idiot tells her ahead of time. Do you really want to spend the entire time we were supposed to be cooking together arguing about this? Because you know that's what's going to happen."

There was a pause.

"You're right. I don't care if you get yourself bitten, barbecued, and chewed up by a Dragon. If that's how you want to die, be my guest. But only if you compromise. Here's clothes for today." Lily threw something at Dahlia.

The outfit was very cute, probably far too cute to spend cooking in a hot kitchen, but Dahlia did like to dress up just like her sister and mother and grandmother. No reason you couldn't look cute while cooking.

"So did you catch him?" Her sister asked casually. "Your mark— is that you call it?"

"What mark?"

"The guy." Her sister's voice climbed an octave. "You know. From last night. The one who was a real beast who just kept going and going."

"Him." Dahlia remembered his face, so gorgeous and yet so strangely innocent and empty of any thought. Pure male animal. "No. He got away."

But at least so did I.

Her sister, an Empath like Dahlia, picked up the unspoken thought and her eyes became wide as ceramic bowls. "By the Light! He was hunting you, wasn't he? Is there any chance he followed you home? Is he going to hunt the rest of us to? Dahlia, I warned you over and over again this might happen one day. You are a rabbit. *You are prey.* You are not a huntress. Predators hunt us!"

"It's fine. I'm fine. No one followed me. I can turn myself invisible, remember?"

"One of these days," her sister said quietly, "It's not going to be fine. You're going to meet a predator who turns the tables and hunt you and doesn't stop until he catches you. And you'll be lucky if the only thing he does is eat you."

Five

September 9
Sunrise: 06:44
Sunset: 19:24
Moon: Full Moon -1
Daylight: 12:39 hours

ALMOST A FULL WEEK of school had passed and Aaresh was doing no better at maintaining discipline in the classroom.

If anything, just the opposite. The kids had decided he was a lightweight. He had looked in at other teachers' classrooms and seen the kids sitting quietly, focused on their work at their desks.

In his classroom, the kids for some reason decided they had the right to race around the room, throw things at each other, play on their phones.... One couple even started to make out in the corner.

The principal, after observing only a few minutes,

returned to hand Aaresh a paper with suggested discipline techniques. He had tried all of them and they were completely useless. None of the items on the list mentioned electroshock therapy.

Eating one of the students as a lesson to the others was looking more and more promising.

One of the marks of maturity, civilization, and power among Shifters was the issue of whether one had control of one's animal form. Many shifters, especially the young, like his students, lost control when they changed into their animal. Worse, when they became an animal, they became that animal completely, with no ability to retain their human thoughts. This was what led to unfortunate events such as Wolf Shifters attacking humans in the woods, and then some teenager waking up with blood on his chin and his clothes missing, wondering what the hell he had done during the night.

Demi-shifters, such as Centaurs, Werewolves, Naagfas, Mermaids, and so on, retained a human element even in their alter form. They didn't ever completely become an animal, although they, too, could suffer from a loss of control as the form influenced their emotions and made them more aggressive or alluring depending on the type of magic.

When Aaresh had applied for this teaching job, the first thing he had been tested on was control in his animal form. Principal Mercado did not mind that he used a very sophisticated illusion to hide what he was, as long as she knew the truth. and she knew that in his lion form he had perfect control.

What he hadn't told her was his dirty little secret.

He didn't have perfect control of his other alter at all. But his alter form wasn't a lion.

While Aaresh had been downward spiraling into a drain of his own self-recrimination, the noise level in the class had been approaching Ragnarök levels. He roused himself once again to try to restore order.

"I need everyone to quiet down now," he said.

No one even heard him over the noise.

"Class, I'm serious. Kids, come out that's enough. Time to… Don't do that, Brian. Brian, I said sit down. Class I need you to…"

Even as he struggled to plant them down, Brian Hatch, a 13 year-old Wolverine Shifter switched completely into his animal form. It wasn't too surprising. The full moon was only one day away, and the Shifters started changing to one to three days before that. Teenage boys might lose control an entire week before the full moon and for an entire week afterward. It wasn't as common during the day, but it happened.

And it was happening right now, in his classroom. Brian turned into a wolverine and started chasing Terry Oakleaf, a helpless Squirrel Shifter. She screamed and shifted as well. Just like the wolves, shifters of every type had stronger magic toward the full moon and weaker magic toward the new moon.

All of the other kids were going wild. Aaresh had a terrible premonition that Brian was going to either snap Terry's neck, or worse, shift back into human form, and start tearing her clothes off.

And Aaresh would be responsible for the assault, not the out-of-control child.

Aaresh didn't know what to do. Should he kill Brian before he raped Terry? How would he explain that to Brian's parents? But if he let Brian harm Terry, how did he explain that to *her* parents?

Suddenly his own temper exploded, and he roared.

He didn't just roar.

He ROARED.

The glamour couldn't disguise the sound of a Shamash, a Sun Lion, bellowing a direct challenge to battle. Even worse, Aaresh had let a spark of his magic slip into the roar, adding a fierce note of *Compulsion to Fear* to the sound. It was possible for a Shamash to kill his enemies from the atavistic fright induced by his roar alone. Aaresh had to be more careful.

Brian and Terry instantaneously popped back into the human form. They and every other student in the class cringed and fell silent.

They all cowered before him in terror.

"Now," said Aaresh calmly. "Everyone, resume your seats. I don't want to hear *a single word* out of any of you the rest of this class period."

The students hurried back to their desks, their jaws clamped tightly shut. Only Terry said something as she passed him, whispering, "Thanks Mr Raj! I didn't even know a Centaur could make a sound like that!"

Thank goodness his illusion had not been broken. And yet, at some level, every student had recognized, deeper than their conscious cognition, that he was not a harmless half-horse half-nerd professor, but a top predator. He saw the fear reflected in their eyes and he felt ashamed, even though he also felt relieved because he could finally give his exciting lecture on Ovid and Metamorphosis.

"Ovid," said Aaresh happily, "was a Roman Shapeshifter, a Faun, as it happens, who wrote stories for humans about our kind... Of course, he changed some of the details to be deliberately absurd so as to protect the shape shifters he knew personally, but we can still read his stories and discover interesting things about Shifter history here in the Mundane sphere..."

~

Aaresh had been so afraid of behaving like the worst abusers in the laboratory where he was raised that he had been afraid to use any discipline at all. But even though he had threatened the kids a little, he hadn't hurt anyone. And it was so much more pleasant to teach after he had their quiet attention and respect.

He decided to repeat the experiment, when necessary, when the noise level rose, and pretty soon, he had every single class sitting quietly in their seats listening as he talked. He even enjoyed his Junior and Senior class at the end of the day.

He found himself sharing some of his excitement about literature with them. He wanted to show them that this was not just a boring subject they had to get through until they could go run in the woods in the moonlight, throwing off their human intelligence and behaving like animals.

"As a Shifter, you may not have telepathy," remarked Aaresh. "You may not have a powerful animal. Maybe you're even human and don't have the ability to become another creature at all. There are a few people in the school who don't have any magic and yet are still studying it. And I am telling you, even if you are the most mundane human, you can find all the magic you want, just waiting for you—in the library. *Books are magic.* Through books, you can escape into another life. Through books, you can become a different person.

"It doesn't matter how terrible your own family is, you can live in another family through a book. You can experience good families; you can experience terrible families. It doesn't matter if you've never been to another country, through a book you can travel there. You can learn about a culture that is completely different than your own.

"Even if you were raised in a cave, or a cage, underground, by people who hated you, you could still find love, and know what it is and how it works, by finding it in a book. And once you have that knowledge, no one can take it from you."

"But book knowledge isn't real knowledge," challenged one of the seniors. "It's just... Academic."

"Of course, it's real knowledge," Aaresh said fiercely. "Someone had to live it, do it, before they could write it down. And the fact that you can read what they wrote gives you the chance to live it, to think it, and do it. The knowledge is on the page, and you still have to transfer it to your life, you have to shape shift those words into flesh. But that doesn't mean it's not real. Words are as real as your bones and blood. It's like music. Music also has its own written language. That sheet of music is real music. Yes, it still requires a musician to put an instrument to his lips or strum his fingers along the strings or pound the drums and bring that music to life. But it's real, it's there, and you can use it to bring light into your life no matter how much darkness you think you have to deal with."

The bell rang and the kids raced out. Their faces went completely blank as soon as they left the class, as if they hadn't absorbed a single word he had said. Maybe he was just talking to himself, he thought.

Still, all in all, it had been a fantastic day. He felt much more confident about the glamour. Maybe it was time to test the illusion in a crowd. Not just a crowd of humans, but a place populated by many other arcanes. If his glamour was going to fail, he wanted to find out now. Before he invested too much in his life, he could run away and start a new life somewhere else, maybe only among humans.

But he didn't want to do that. As dangerous as it was for him, he wanted to stay in Arcana Glen where there were many of his own kind that he could study and learn from and talk to. And when he was ready, he would find a way to do the two things he most wanted: punish those who had hurt him and reconnect with his lost sister. Meanwhile...

He didn't want to be alone.

There was a festival coming up at Dragon Mountain soon. If he could hide his true nature from Dragons, he thought it would work against anyone.

Six

September 10
Sunrise: 06:45
Sunset: 19:22
Moon: Full Moon
Daylight: 12:37 hours

THE AREA in front of Dragon Mountain was usually just a clearing. The caves were a tourist attraction, and the caves were open as usual, but this was not a good day to go if you were just an ordinary out-of-town tourist. Hundreds of locals had turned up for the street food, acrobats and entertainment, contests and games that were all part of the Autumn Twilight Festival celebrated by Shifters from Autumndelle and Springvale.

The Enchanted Circus, which worked with the Magician and usually performed at the casino next to the Castle, always sent performers to local Arcana Glen fairs and festivals. Today, they were performing a dance based on the legend of the Bunny Shifter and the Tiger Shifter, in theory to honor the Year of the Tiger. The tiger in the story was the bad guy, however, who chased a Rabbit Shifter. The Rabbit Shifter created a rope out of the sea and climbed to the moon. It was the same story that had inspired Dahlia to find the real spell that had inspired the legend. She didn't really climb past the atmosphere, but she could see why it might look like that to the Tiger left to prowl helplessly on the ground as his prey disappeared into a cloud of invisibility.

Dahlia had agreed to serve food from the booth that advertised her family's restaurant, *Bao & Bun*. Most Rabbit Shifters, like her family, focused on cooking moon cakes and other food for the spirits who came to visit their descendants. These moon cakes contained a special form of Light magic that enabled spirits to eat the spiritual part of the cake, while humans could eat the physical part, which was a mix of mundane food and Elemental magic. A spirit who ate the cake became half-way manifest in the physical world. A human who ate the cake became able to see such ghosts. That was the magic of the festival. Ancestors could descend from the higher Three Realms and visit their descendants.

Normally, Dahlia couldn't see ghosts, but today she could. Ancestor spirits, glowing shapes illuminated from within like paper lanterns, thronged the streets as well as humans. Needless to say, the Moon family had ancestors by the dozen, all of whom felt the need to stop by the altar at the back of the booth, devour the spirit half of the moon cakes, and then give long-winded speeches on how the current generation of Moons were a disappointment to the family, along with copious amounts of advice how to rectify this situation.

Great-great-grandmother asked Dahlia's mother, "Why did you let Dahlia become a bodyguard?"

"Bounty-hunter, not bodyguard," Dahlia muttered.

Mother shushed her. "Show respect to the Ancestors!" She bowed to Great-great-grandmother and said, "I know this well, Granny. I told her to become a doctor!"

"A doctor?" scoffed Great-great-grandmother. "Why work so hard? With her face, she could have been the concubine of a mighty Elf Lord!"

Dahlia rolled her eyes. She edged away from the conversation at the back of the booth, to engage the living customers instead.

However, there was another side to the Autumn Twilight Festival.

The more aggressive predators use the Autumn Twilight Festival as a chance to test each other's metal and recruit new warriors. Dahlia scanned the crowd looking for Logan. The White Wolf Shifter had agreed to enter the contest with her. Every year there were contests at the twilight festival. In the past, the Elven Kings and Queens sponsored the contests, looking for Knights for the different Elemental Elven Courts. Shifter Alphas sought hunters to recruit into their packs. Here in Arcana Glen, the Autumn Twilight Festival served as an impromptu job fair for every sort of arcane career.

This was Dahlia's chance to prove to some of the top Shifters and most powerful mages in Arcana Glen that if they ever needed a bounty hunter, they should come to her directly. In order to be taken seriously, though, she had to make an impression.

The strongest Shifters of any kind, from any realm, were Dragons. And the strongest Dragon was the Empress, Victoria Long. She was both the Queen of her own Dragon

Clan and a Guardian, respected by the wizards and witches of the human magic community, as well as by the Elves. If Dahlia could impress the Empress, Dahlia would automatically impress everyone else as well.

As the Empress was the top of the top predators, even she had to constantly prove her strength to her own people —and to her enemies. Some detractors had been spreading sly rumors that her marriage, in March, to a human man, had weakened her. Even though her mate was a Dragon Slayer, with his own fearsome reputation, not to mention, the Emperor Guardian, he was human.

Therefore, the Empress and the Emperor had declared they would accept challenges from any other couple to fight in an arena. The challenges were done two against two to avoid the danger of someone challenging her to steal her husband, which was not that uncommon among Dragon females, who could be quite fierce; or the reverse, to avoid someone challenging her husband to win her and replace the Emperor on the throne. That was quite common among Dragons as well, and very common among other Shifters.

Sure, it wasn't common among *Bunny* Shifters. But lots of other types.

Dahlia had never met the Dragon Empress, but once, Troy Stern, the Emperor, had stopped by her family's restaurant to order catering. Apparently, he enjoyed Korean food. He wasn't pretentious or vainglorious but behaved like the guy next door. Her empathy could pick up that his humility was genuine, not feigned. She'd have had no idea who he was, except she recognized his magic ring.

Anyone who thought that the Emperor would be easy to defeat in one-on-one combat just because he was a human was very foolish and ignorant, thought Dahlia.

She'd studied up on him after he stopped by. He was one of those humans who have been born without any magic, yet just through the purity of his heart and the strength of his character, had been called to become a Hero and a Slayer of rabid monsters. He had been granted many magical objects that gave him power equal to any of his foes. He had a magic ring, a magic sword, a magic shield... and probably other things as well that she knew nothing about for good security reasons. Maybe, like Dahlia, he was happy to let his enemies underestimate him.

The Empress had powers that were considerable as well. However, no one made the mistake of underestimating the Dragon Empress. Just being in her presence was enough to make humans and even Shifters freeze in terror. There was even a name for it: *dragon-fear*.

Last year, one of the most embarrassing contests had occurred when a Bear Shifter had challenged Victoria Long, who was then not even a Guardian yet, but a mere Princess; but when face-to-face with her he had become completely paralyzed. Completely. He had to be dragged physically out of the arena.

Please don't let that happen to me, Dahlia thought. As a Yuetu Rabbit Shifter, freezing in fear in the face of a predator was already an instinctual response. Add to it the fact that a Dragon could make even another top predator freeze in fright, and it was no wonder her friends and family thought Dahlia was crazy to want to challenge the Empress.

Her sister knew exactly what she was thinking.

"Don't do it," Lily said.

"I have to at least try," Dahlia said. Neither of them needed to specify what they were talking about. And they both glanced conspiratorially at their mother. If she knew, she would go ballistic. Talk about a dangerous rabbit.

"Being able to change into a small size is an advantage," Dahlia said softly, "Remember when..."

"When the bear froze, how could I forget?"

"I was going to say, when the Cat Girl fought the Empress at the Circus try-outs in May? Remember how she turned into a little tiny cat and used her tiny size to her advantage? I studied that fight, and my technique is a little different but basically relies on the same principle. By being able to shift into a small animal in the arena against a big animal, I have a huge advantage."

"Until she steps on you. And you can't compare yourself to a cat. Even a house cat is still a predator, Dahlia," Lily pointed out. "She might be able to become small, but, by the way, she also can turn into a lioness, and either way she has that predatory instinct to run towards danger."

"And my instinct is to fight like water. Seek to be where I am not expected, turn my opponent's strength against him—"

"You also seem to forget that the cat-shifter turned out to be a Guardian. *You* are not a Guardian," Lily said crushingly. "You're nothing close to a Guardian. I know you're a great bounty hunter, but most of your technique still involves running away from the people you're supposed to be hunting. Basically, your entire plan always comes around to using yourself as bait."

"And it works pretty well."

"Until it doesn't. Sometimes the shark gets away with the fish on the hook."

Her sister held up a plate of colorful moon-shaped cakes. "All I'm saying is, no one ever died fighting a moon cake. I don't want to lose you."

"Look, there's Logan! I have to talk to him about the fight. If it bothers you too much, don't watch."

"'Don't watch,' she tells *me*... her sister!" Lily rolled her eyes. "Of course I'm going to watch! I'll probably have a heart attack and die, but I'm going to watch!"

Dahlia took off her apron and hurried after Logan.

~

"Logan! I thought you were going to come see me at my booth."

"Dahlia." The handsome Wolf Shifter shook his head. "I'm sorry. I should've... The truth is I totally forgot. I'm not here on pleasure, I am here on business." Logan gestured to Yuri Lojka, the Vampire. The big, tatted-up Vampire looked bored.

"Go haf fun with Bunny girl," urged Yuri. "Don't vorry about me. I von't bite anyone."

"No," said Logan. "I told you, Vampire, I'm your shadow. Get used to it."

Yuri snorted. Whistling, which sounded weird because of his fangs, he wandered away.

"So..." Dahlia said, her heart sinking, "You aren't going to partner with me in the contest."

Logan grimaced. "Unfortunately, yeah, the timing isn't really ideal, believe me. I'm sorry, but I can't. I have to stick to the Vampire like glue. Maybe next year, okay?"

"But you promised. Can't you get one of the other Rangers to take your shift?"

"Dahlia, this is work. For me being a Ranger is an *actual job*. It's not just a hobby like Bounty Hunting is for you."

Her sister had told her to stop punching single handsome men, but this was another one of those times that Dalia was going to have to ignore her advice. However, before Dahlia could show how furious she was at his casual insult, Logan hurried away after Yuri before the Vampire could disappear into the crowd.

Dahlia was so furious that tears sprang to her eyes. Ugh! This was another thing she hated about being a Rabbit Shifter. Or maybe it was being a hormonal female, like her dad claimed. Or maybe she was just cursed. She cried so easily. Hot tears turned everything around her to water. She blinked furiously trying to hold the tears back. How pathetic was it to cry like a baby because she wasn't going to get to be in a fight?

Yeah, that was really going to convince everyone to take her seriously.

She could barely see where she was going in the crowd until she collided with a broad masculine chest. Unlike most of the people at the festival, who were dressed casually, this man was wearing a suit, but he was huge, very wide across the shoulders and very tall. Muscles like boulders hid under that urbane wardrobe. Strong arms steadied her and even lifted her a little off the ground and set her back on her feet.

Seven

September 10
Sunrise: 06:45
Sunset: 19:22
Moon: Full Moon
Daylight: 12:37 hours

THE TIPS of Dahlia's ears burned with humiliation at how easily the stranger picked her up and set her back on the pavement. She looked up. And up. Finally, she saw why he was so tall. He was a centaur. He had strong masculine features, and eyes that sparkled with intelligence behind wire rim glasses. At first, she thought he had short dark hair, but then she saw it was tied back in a ponytail at the nap of his neck. He was clean-shaven, but obviously fighting nature, because he already had the stubble of a 5 o'clock shadow even though it was only 11 o'clock in the morning.

There was also something strangely familiar about him. Dark hair, chiseled face, golden skin... Her face heated when she realized he reminded her of the Wild Man who had followed her in the woods. But the resemblance was only skin deep. The Wild Man and the Centaur both had the same tone of gleaming skin and dark hair but the Centaur's mind blazed like a shining sun to her Empathy.

He was a genius, this man, and highly skilled in a number of fields. Her Empathy didn't tell her what, exactly, only that his mind was a splendid edifice, like the Greek Parthenon: elegant, classic, strong, graceful and rational.

The fact that he had attended a street fair wearing a blazer, vest and dress shirt and the fact that he wore glasses even though he was a Demi-shifter and probably had perfect vision, made him look extremely nerdy and a little out of place. But there was something familiar about his scent. It was horsey and... yet possessed an odd tang of something else...

She snapped her fingers. "You teach at Arcana Academy, don't you?"

He blinked. Behind the glasses, those eyes were absolutely gorgeous, like polished agate, a swirl of golden specks against shadows of sienna and umber.

"How do you know that? Are you a teacher there?"

"I am! Well," she amended quickly, "Not actually at the Academy. I share a classroom with you. I am the night schoolteacher who uses that space from 8 to 11 at night. Dahlia Moon."

"Oh! Oh, that is you. Fancy meeting you here of all places." He shook her hand. "Aaresh Raj."

"We aren't likely to run into each other at the school, are we?" She chuckled. "But I recognized your smell."

"You're a Shifter," he said cautiously.

Some Demi-shifters, especially those with herbivore animals, like horses, were wary around full Animal Shifters.

For the first time in her life, she found herself wanting to reassure him that she was a Yuetu, just a harmless Rabbit Shifter. But she bit her lip. She was trying to prove to the world that she *wasn't* harmless; she couldn't just turn around when it was convenient and fall back on that stereotype.

Besides, Centaurs were not as harmless as they looked either. He was one huge stallion, and he didn't get those muscles just flipping pages. She was willing to bet that his glasses were magical, if they served any use, because there was no way he needed to adjust his vision. Centaurs were notorious for their excellent vision, and both near and far.

"My family has a booth selling moon cakes back there. Come with me and I'll get you some food. Have you eaten lunch yet?"

"No," he admitted. "I've never had moon cakes."

"Never?"

"This is my first time at this festival. It's... It's a little overwhelming. There are so many more people than I thought."

"Oh, this is nothing, you should see the New Year's parade in February. Or maybe you've been to that?"

"I'm new to... Arcana Glen."

Just a slight pause made Dahlia wonder if he meant something more significant. "Oh? Did you just come from another Sphere?"

"I was born and raised here, but my family kept me separated from the rest of society. Homeschooled and all of that."

"Were they afraid humans would find out what you really were? I don't know why so many Shifter families are afraid of that. My sister tells every human she meets that she's a Yuetu, and they just never believe her." Dahlia didn't add that Lily usually managed to get the men in the sack with that line about being a Bunny.

"They were very private people and extremely dysfunctional on top of that. I have been forced to learn what few social skills I have from books and cinema, so I apologize if I make any mistakes. Please blame pop-culture."

If one of those mistakes included dressing like an Edwardian gentleman on the fine autumn day, she thought, he could do worse.

Aaresh had recognized the other teacher's smell right away but had held himself back from saying so because he was not supposed to be a full Shifter. Centaurs were supposed to have a good eyesight, but not necessarily great smell, since their noses were human.

As a Shamash, however, Aaresh had instantly determined she was a Yuetu. He had been afraid that as a prey animal, she would be better able to pierce his illusion than others. Her defensive instinct might overwhelm the glamour and warn her that he was dangerous. But instead of running away from him, she invited him back to her booth.

She introduced him to her sister and her mother, who were both beautiful, although not as beautiful as she was. Aaresh couldn't get over how adorable she was, with her swinging black pigtails, her khaki shorts and tank top.

Calm down, boy, he warned himself. She's not yours. She could never be yours.

He would never be able to take a mate because of the problem with his shifting. And he would never be able to explain to any interested woman why he had to reject her, because he couldn't reveal his condition without explaining what had been done to him, and by whom. That would mean revealing that he was a mutant from a laboratory, the escaped property of a secret organization.

Anyone who found out the truth would have one of two reactions. On the one hand, evil-hearted people might try to take advantage of the knowledge by contacting the organization looking for him and accepting money to turn him over to them. On the other hand, a hypothetical good-hearted person would be put in danger trying to protect him. Anyone who knew his secret would risk being targeted by the organization as well. Either way, he didn't dare tell the truth.

He hated lies, but he had no choice. In essence, the people who had raised him in a cage had ensured that he would never be able to be truly free. He would always live in a cage of lies.

Dahlia piled food onto his plate, and although Aaresh tried to make a token protest, everything was so delicious that he found himself stuffing his face. As a Shifter, he had a tremendous appetite and he had been feeling peckish before she found him, so this was a delight. He kept praising the cooks and earned big smiles from her mother and her sister.

However, Dalia herself dragged him away eventually so she could talk to him in private.

"You seem quite physically fit for an academic," she remarked.

He glanced at her sidelong.

"I'm betting there's a side of you that you don't share with your fifth-grade students," she said.

"Most of my students are a little older than that."

"I guess that makes sense if you're teaching *Twelfth Night*. 'Conceal me what I am, and be my aid for such disguise as haply shall become the form of my intent.' That's what you're teaching right now, isn't it?"

His face lit up. "You know your Shakespeare. My favorite line is, 'I say there is no darkness but ignorance.' Alas, we won't get to that until later in the year. Right now, we're on Ovid."

"Metamorphosis," she said.

He radiated sheer delight. "Yes."

"I love reading," she said. "But I also do martial arts. What about you?"

He hesitated. He had been forced to learn to fight, along with all the other things he had learned as a child. But he didn't *like* to do it. The people who raised him had been so impressed with his physical strength that whenever they wanted to punish one of the other Shifters, they put that person alone in a cell with Aaresh. The idea was that he would kill the Shifter in combat. He never wanted to do it, but the frightened Shifters usually attacked Aaresh first, leaving him no choice but to defend himself.

The fact that Aaresh was alive was proof he'd never lost a fight.

"I do know *how* to fight," he said, "But I am a peace-loving man."

"This isn't anything that will hurt anyone or anything like that," she said quickly. "It's just that... This is going to sound crazy, but I need a huge favor."

She was practically bouncing on the balls of her feet in her nervousness. Her two pigtails were bobbing on top of her head like floppy bunny ears, and she looked up at him with such huge pleading eyes that if she had asked him to cut out his own heart and hand it to her at that moment, he would've gladly done so.

"My friend left me in a lurch. He promised to join me

in one of the contests today, but then he had to work, and he backed out. The contest requires a team of two, a male and female partner. If I don't find a male partner between now and..." She checked her watch, "Fifteen minutes from now, I can't enter the contest at all, I have to wait another whole year. No one gets hurt, it's just for fun. Just to show what you can do. I can't enter alone. It doesn't matter if we win or not, I just really want to enter this contest. Would you be my partner?"

"Yes," he said.

"Great! You... uh... better take off your jacket. And your shirt. And your glasses. The contest will be held inside Dragon Mountain, because we're going to be going up against the Empress and the Emperor."

"Wait... What?!"

What had he gotten himself into?

Dahlia felt sorry for Aaresh—he looked *so* embarrassed to remove his clothes.

She pointed out that a blazer was not going to be very practical for a fight involving hand to hand combat, as well as possible projectile magic like balls of flame. He agreed, but at the last minute, he put his vest back on over his bare chest.

"I just can't stand to go naked like an animal," he said apologetically. "I don't care if the vest gets ruined in the fight."

Considering he was being a great sport to partner her in a fight fifteen minutes before it was supposed to start, when they had never actually met in person before, she wasn't going to complain about his peccadillos.

However, bashfulness was not his only quirk.

They joined the crowd streaming toward the entrance into the caverns below Dragon Mountain, but abruptly, Aaresh dug in his heels and stopped moving. "Wait. Don't tell me the fight is being held underground?"

"Don't tell me you're afraid of the dark," she joked.

But the look he gave her sent chills down her spine. He was very afraid of something. Maybe not of the dark... maybe of Dragons?

"It's not dark in there," Dahlia said. "And no one is going to..."

Well, she couldn't say no one would *hurt* him, because people did get hurt in the fights, "No one is going to kill you. It's not a fight to the death, it's just for fun."

For her it was about a lot more than fun but piling on the stakes didn't seem like the right move. Dammit, she should've known it was too easy to find a replacement for Logan. This nerd had phobias up the wazoo. How was he going to fight Dragons if he was afraid to even walk into the cave?

Ahead of them, a huge stone gate, looking like the massive stone and bronze door of an ancient oriental palace, had been set across the entrance of the cave. People disappeared as they entered the mouth of the cave, not into the darkness, but into thin air.

A sign in English and the Ancient Dragon pictorial language explained: Enter the Gate at Your Own Peril, for Beyond This Threshold, You Enter Autumndelle.

"Look!" Dahlia pointed. "We're not even going into the mountain itself. We're going through a portal into another realm. Probably the Sphere of Autumndelle."

Traveling to an arcane Sphere somewhere else in the

multiverse should have been more frightening than going into a cave, but Aaresh looked excited.

"So it's true! Now that the Guardians are returning, the Gates between the Spheres are opening again!"

"I heard the rumor that the war of liberation in Autumndelle has begun," Dahlia said. "The Winter Elves have been driven back from the capital, although they maintain a foothold in the wild lands."

"Are we really going to travel through a Gate and see it for ourselves?"

"There's only one way to find out," said Dahlia. She held out her hand.

He linked his arm with hers, like the Edwardian gentleman he dressed like, and together, they strolled through the Gate of Shimmering magic.

Eight

September 10
Sunrise: 06:45
Sunset: 19:22
Moon: Full Moon
Daylight: 12:37 hours

DAHLIA AND AARESH emerged into a huge arena under a cerulean sky. The sky itself didn't look so different from the Mundane Sphere, and the arena superficially resembled a Roman amphitheater, a round stadium, tiered with stone arches and stone benches. It was ten times the scale of any Roman edifice, however, and the sandstone and marble glittered with precious metals and glittering gemstones.

And there were arcanes everywhere.

Golden Dragons and Gargoyles flew overhead or perched on the top ledges of the stadium. Dwarves and Gremlins were clearing out the debris from the arena floor:

blood-soaked dirt, shattered weapons, and lost bits of armor. After they finished, a team of Centaurs pulled metal rakes behind them to smooth out the ground which had been torn up in the last fight. The audience in the stone tiers consisted mostly of Autumn Elves (Glamir), Dwarves, Gargoyles, and Gnomes with a smattering of Goblins, Witches, Werewolves, Gorgons, Dryads and so many others that Dahlia couldn't guess them all.

Space in the rows of stone seats had been cordoned off for the newcomers from Mundania. Dahlia and Aaresh shuffled along with the rest of the gawkers. Those from Earth had either never been to Autumndelle before or had not been there in at least ten years. Everyone was gazing around, trying to drink in the sights, just like Dahlia and Aaresh.

Aaresh's eyes were full of wonder already, but his gaze arrested on a figure directly across from them. It was an immense stone lion statue, the kind one saw guarding palaces and cities, even in Mundania. Four of these immense stone lions sat on pedestals at each of the four points of the compass in the middle of the tiers, like watch dogs.

One of the stone lions swished his tail. Another flicked her ear.

They weren't statues, Dahlia realized. They were like the Gargoyles, so imbued with Elemental Stone magic that they appeared to be made of living stone in their alter forms.

"The Shishi: the Great Stone Lion Shifters of Autumn-delle. I've only heard of them. I've never been off the Mundane Sphere before," Aaresh admitted.

"Me neither."

"It's amazing that it's so easy to just walk through a portal to another plane of existence!"

"Not so easy," she said. "For a long time, no one could travel at all between the Spheres because all the Guardians were dead. Only the Emperor and Empress, or another Guardian, could have opened this Gate."

The arriving guests from Mundania started to settle down on the stone benches to watch the next fight. Dahlia bounced on the balls of her feet, twitching.

"We're in the wrong place," she said. "We're with the spectators, but we need to go find out where the Challengers wait to enter the arena. I don't know how we're going to find anything in this stadium. It looks like it was designed by Giants."

Aaresh and Dahlia struggled to thread the crowd and find someone who could direct them where to go. She was right about the size of the stadium. It was huge, as if designed for opening night at the Olympics or a soccer game in Brazil. There were thousands upon thousands of people in the stands, all mythical creatures he had only read about in books.

He wished he were here to wander the stacks of the Great Library of the University of Autumndelle, to listen to the sunset serenades of the Glamir Elves, to watch the Dryads dance at dawn to honor the rising sun, anything, rather than to fight someone. But he was glad that the sun was shining overhead, that he wasn't underground, which would remind him of the laboratory and triggered a panic rage and possibly even cause him to shift to his other, dangerous form. He could keep his promise to the beautiful Rabbit Shifter.

Besides, Aaresh had read so many books about the gladiatorial events in Rome that he couldn't help a little thrill at seeing something very similar come to life before his eyes.

A deep, joyful male voice cried out, "Aaresh!"

Aaresh and Dahlia both looked around for the man who had spoken, but they didn't see him until he finally emerged from the crowd, for he was a Dwarf, two heads shorter even than Dahlia. He had broad shoulders, a handsome face and a full beard and he wore Mundane clothes, a biker's black leather jacket over blue jeans. Chains rattled at his waist. The Dwarf was dressed quite differently than the conservative suits he usually wore, but Aaresh recognized him.

"Erik! I didn't expect to see you here!" Aaresh gestured to Dahlia. "Dahlia, this is Erik Orecoat, a fellow teacher at the Academy. Erik, this is Dahlia Moon. She teaches night school."

"Are you both here for the Guardian trials?" asked Erik.

"Uh... I hope not," said Aaresh, glancing at Dahlia. Surely she would have told him if that were the contest she wanted to enter?

Even someone as socially isolated as Aaresh had heard about the revival of the Guardians. After ten years of all but one of the positions being empty, suddenly–supposedly– new Guardians were "Called" by twos every month. At first, it had seemed random, but now there was a definite pattern and the Guardians held open auditions. Aaresh harbored deep suspicions about the whole endeavor. The flood of new Guardians was just too pat, too convenient. And what did they want with his sister? What hold did they have over her that forced her to work for them?

"No, we aren't auditioning to become Guardians," said Dahlia. "We're here for a different challenge, to take on the Emperor and Empress in hand-to-hand combat. But tell me about the Guardian trials... are they also going to take place in the arena?"

Erik laughed. "I doubt the trial to find the Guardian of the Tower, a position usually held by an Engineer, or the Guardian of the Star, a position usually held by an artist, are going to involve combat in the arena. I'm here to try my hand at becoming Guardian of the Tower, but the first step was signing an NDA, so even after the trial, I won't be able to tell you."

"Good luck," said Aaresh. He tried to sound sincere, although the idea of someone who knew him joining the Guardians made Aaresh uneasy. They already had some hold over his sister. Now they were recruiting teachers from the Academy? He didn't like it.

"Thanks, although I don't have a snowball's chance in Darkpyre," said Erik Orecoat cheerfully. "I heard that the leading contender is the Defector."

"What Defector?" asked Aaresh.

"One of the Azir princes defected recently," said Dahlia. "I believe it was Prince Venamor, who was notorious for inventing magical weapons for the war. He shocked everyone by helping in the liberation of Autumndelle."

"That's right, so he has a lot of characteristics going for him for Guardian of the Tower," said Erik. "He's an engineer but a rebel, a prince but a spy. Great stuff."

"Sure, but the Light has a way of surprising us," said Dahlia. "Who knows who will get Called or why? I'm sure you still have a chance, Erik."

Erik beamed at her, and Aaresh also cast her a sidelong glance, aware that kindness as much as conviction had spurred her encouraging statement. Still, perhaps she sympathized with the Dwarf who wanted to be a Guardian, because she was a Bunny Shifter who wanted to fight a Dragon. She must be used to others scoffing at her dreams. Aaresh felt a rush of admiration that she had not let it either embitter her or lead her to belittle others.

They wished Erik good luck again and parted ways, threading the crowd until they came to the floor level of the arena. A Glamir, an Elf with acorn-toned skin, chestnut brown hair, and topaz gold eyes, directed them to a ramp that brought them to the floor of the arena, in a stone chamber right outside the ring. A Dwarf there confirmed that Dahlia "plus one," was registered to fight in an upcoming match.

Aaresh swallowed. This was happening. He hoped he didn't let her down.

Everything happened swiftly after that. They were allowed their pick of weapons and armor from a rack against the wall. Dahlia selected several weapons and then slipped them into the ether, the void between worlds.

Other couples were there, each pair waiting their turn to tilt against the reigning champions. The Dwarf waved each pair through a stone portcullis, and beyond. Dahlia and Aaresh watched through a grille as the matches before them played out.

The opponents met in the center of the amphitheater. The Empress was already in her dragon form, shining ruby flanks and obsidian dorsal scales. Her scales had been decorated with golden lace and diamonds. The Emperor, in shining armor, rode on her back in a great, golden saddle. He balanced a huge lance on a brace mounted upon the saddle.

Turn by turn, pairs of challengers entered the arena and fought with them.

It didn't seem very fair to Aaresh because they had to fight challenger after challenger. Weren't they getting tired? Whereas each set of challengers was fresh and eager to prove themselves.

However, the huge scarlet Dragon and her husband in golden armor defeated all of the other couples who tried to fight them without any trouble. Some of the fights were extremely short, in fact. Most challengers were dispatched in a matter of minutes.

After nineteen other couples had entered the arena before them and come out on stretchers, Aaresh said to Dahlia, "Are you certain this is a great idea?"

He wondered if she expected him to carry most of the fight, given that she was only a cute little Bunny Shifter. If so, she had picked the wrong guy. His loathing of aggression meant that he had focused most of his life on defensive fighting.

Dahlia flashed a grin. She was bouncing with excitement. Her pigtails bobbed.

"It's our turn!" she said, "Let's go out there and just do our best, okay?" She touched his arm. "Thank you for doing this, Aaresh."

Aw, he couldn't resist that. Even if he came out on a stretcher. He grimaced and walked with her through the portcullis to face the Dragon and Champion.

Aaresh and Dahlia emerged into the sunlit arena. The portcullis clanged shut behind them. Suddenly Aaresh had a last-minute inspiration. "Get on my back. You can ride can't you?"

"Yes," she said. She leapt lightly onto his back. As he expected she weighed no more than a bit of fluff resting in the small of his back. He hoped that glamour would convince her if she was riding on a centaur and not on a lion. The gaits of a horse and a feline were quite different, not to mention his shape was different. But when she wrapped her arms around his chest, he felt it as if she were actually touching his human skin.

That was one reason he had chosen this form for his illusion. He couldn't be himself in his human body; this was as close as he could get. The human half of his centaur body was modeled on his actual features and physique of a man, and the tactile dimension of the glamour meant that he felt like he had human skin when she touched him. So much so that he had felt embarrassed going bare-chested in front of her. In front of anyone, really. He had an absolute loathing of anything animalistic or primitive in himself.

He galloped out into the arena. The red Dragon attacked instantly, diving from the sky, bombarding them with fire. Okay, then. Apparently even in this friendly little "fun" fight, the Dragon was holding nothing back.

And then huge fat black arrows begin to fall from the sky. The arrows were enchanted and chased them around like heat-seeking missiles. The Emperor was no slouch either.

Aaresh darted out of the way of the fire, twisting his body with the flexibility of his hidden feline self. The maneuver probably looked amazing coming from a horse. He had to be careful not to reveal himself. Better to lose the fight than to give away his secret.

That might not be fair to Dahlia, but he had to protect himself above all.

He couldn't evade the arrows, but when they came close, he allowed a corona of fire to surround his body and the arrows burned up before they could reach him. He included Dahlia inside the corona, so she wasn't harmed.

"Awesome!" she cried. His ponytail had come undone, and his hair was flying free in the air. "You have Elemental Fire! Can you shoot at the wings, force the Dragon to land?"

He was about to apologize that he only had a shield, no weapons of offense, but she had already leapt off his back, retrieved one of the arrows that had missed and not been burned up. She pulled a bow from out of the ether where she must have stored it and shot the Emperor's own arrow back at him.

The huge arrow withstood the heat of the Dragon and hit her in the wing when she barrel-rolled to evade a direct hit to her heart.

Aaresh was stunned at Dahlia's audacity.

He regretted being part of this. He had no desire to hurt the beautiful Dragon Empress or her husband, and he had even less desire to provoke attention that defeating a Guardian would surely bring. His goal was to learn about them, not provoke them. He knew his sister, who went by the name Moxie Bridgestone, had been forced to work for them, but he wasn't sure how the Guardians kept her on their leash. Was she a prisoner, a captive, or a slave? Or had they blackmailed her? He refused to believe they had bribed her. She wasn't corrupt. Until he understood what hold the Guardians had over her, he didn't dare approach her. All he knew was that the worst scientist from the laboratory, Dr Rasmu, had tried to force Aaresh to join the Guardians as part of some vile scheme. That was enough for Aaresh to know it was best to stay as far away from the Guardians as possible.

Yet here he was. Doing everything possible to bring himself to their attention...

The Dragon was forced to land because of her injured wing. However, she was far from defeated. His worry had been premature. In fact, he was only able to dodge her attacks a few more moments before she swiped him with a large reptilian paw that was as large as his entire body... His real body, not his imaginary one. Her blow was so forceful, it knocked him from the center of the stadium to the wall.

He heard the crack of a bone breaking. Pain shot through him, but he quickly suppressed it. Dealing with pain, ignoring it, was something he had learned to do growing up because he had so frequently been hurt deliberately during experiments.

His body also healed very fast, fast even for a Shifter. His bone was healing already, and he could have loped back to his feet and careened back into the fight. But his heart wasn't in it. The last thing he wanted to do was draw attention to himself by *winning* this challenge.

So, with a silent apology to Delia, he pretended to be more hurt than he was and lay still against the wall.

Nine

September 10
Sunrise: 06:45
Sunset: 19:22
Moon: Full Moon
Daylight: 12:37 hours

DAHLIA FELT a shot of guilt when she saw the brave Centaur whacked against the wall like a pin knocked aside by a bowling ball. She whispered a silent plea for his forgiveness for dragging him into this brutal duel. If he ever even spoke to her again, she would give him free meals from her family restaurant for the rest of his life.

But meanwhile she was still standing. She evaded a similar swipe from the Dragon's talons by switching to her rabbit form. She was not swifter than the Dragon, even as a bunny, but she was so much smaller and more maneuverable that she was able to run right underneath the beast. For more than fifteen minutes, she was able to drag out the contest simply by evading capture or injury.

But she could see the weakness in her plan. Her sister was right when it came right down to it; her only way to bring an aggressor was to act as bait to lure the predator into a trap. With her water rope, she could escape most creatures. It was possible she would even be able to evade an ordinary Dragon. But she had no way to deliver a decisive blow.

The Empress was also an Elemental Water mage. Dahlia wasn't certain her invisibility spell, which used Elemental Water, or her magic rope, which also used Elemental Water, would work against an Elemental Water sorceress as powerful as or impressive as Empress Victoria Long.

Dahlia didn't even try to employ either spell. She didn't want to give away her tricks to an entire stadium of watchers. Her only offensive weapon was the bow. She could summon more arrows out of the ether, but only the arrows of the Emperor's own weapon were strong enough to work against the Dragon. She was just trying to figure out how to steal more arrows from him when suddenly, two human sized feet landed on either side of her and a sack went down over her body.

She tried to shift back to human form, but it was impossible. The magic sack prevented her from shifting. It was made of all four elements, plus something else that she could sense only as a force that was very strong. It was probably Light magic, but it could have even been Dark magic. Between the Empress and the Emperor, they wielded all the Elements *and* the powers of Light and Darkness.

Trapped, Dahlia had to surrender. The Emperor let her out of the bag when she said the words: "I yield!"

He allowed her to return to human form and bowed to

her. The Dragon Empress shifted into her human form. She also bowed to Dahlia.

"Your partner has already been taken away by the healers," Empress Victoria said. "You fought well, noble Yuetu. I think you have lasted longer against us than any other opponent of today's challenge. If no one bests your time by the end of the day, you and your partner will be today's winners. But there are still many other challengers we have to face"

They all bowed to each other again and Delia hobbled off to seek out the injured Centaur professor. Poor man.

She found him in a subterranean room beneath the stadium. True to his apparent phobia of the dark, he had sought out a sun beam from a skylight and dragged his cot so that it was directly under the ray, a little apart from the other rows of recovering warriors.

She ran to his side. "I'm so sorry you were injured fighting with me."

"Not at all," he said. "I'm fully recovered. The Glamir Healers here are absolutely top-notch. I would love to stay here but I need to get back to Arcana Glen as soon as possible."

"Are you sure?" she asked. "We won't know who the winners of the contest are until after the final challengers have had their turn."

"When is that?" he asked.

"Usually six or seven o'clock. The challenges will go on all day."

"After sunset?"

"It just depends how many challengers there are."

He shook his head. "No, I'm afraid I have to get home. Actually... I am still quite sore despite the broken bone healing. I... uh... I need a good night's rest."

"By the Light, you broke your bone? Which one?"

"Several ribs, a little crack in my cranium, and my femur," shrugged Aaresh. "But those are better now." And then he seemed to remember his need to leave. "I'd still prefer to go home, if you don't mind. I'm sorry I can't wait for the announcement of the winner. I don't think we won anyway, do you?"

She shrugged. "Obviously, we didn't defeat the reigning Champions. It wasn't expected that we would beat two Guardians, so that isn't how the winners are chosen. The Emperor and the Empress themselves can't win. They count the total time in the arena that any team can remain standing."

"You were out there almost forty minutes." He smiled. "You were amazing, Dahlia."

He seemed to mean it. But she couldn't convince him to stay. Maybe he was feeling sore, as he claimed, but she couldn't help but feel there was another reason. Even though she hadn't punched him herself, she had still managed to find a handsome single man and injure him within the first day of their acquaintance.

Her sister was right. She was going to be single for the rest of her damn life.

Although they were in another Sphere, another plane of existence from the earthly universe, the sun and the moon of this realm looked and acted much the same as over Earth. Autumndelle was not a broken land like Winterdom, which had been fractured into a series of shattered shards of frozen turf that floated and collided forever in a raging storm filled with deadly blades of ice and steel. Nor was it a land of eternal summer, like Summerland.

Instead, like Springvale, Autumndelle experienced all four seasons, and the ordinary transitions between day and night associated with each. It was named for the Autumn because the denizens of this realm achieved their greatest power during the autumn months. (In Springvale, it was the opposite.)

Supposedly the realms of Winter and Summer had once been the same before the ambitious magic users had attempted to extend the season they favored to the entire year. The wizards of Winterdom had succeeded, but at the terrible price of breaking up and destroying their universe. The wizards of Summer had almost gone as far, and paid for their hubris by creating the Burning Lands, huge areas of desert where nothing could grow, and even areas where the ground was so hot that rivers of molten rock alternated with pools of boiling mud.

Dahlia contemplated the mysteries of the realms as she waited for the rest of the day's fights to unfold. She wasn't injured, so she returned to the tiers, found her sister, Lily, and watched from there.

Just as in the Olympics, the end of the day concluded with a ceremony in which the copper, bronze and gold winners were brought up to receive their metals. (Arcanes didn't give out silver medals because silver was poisonous to so many magical creatures.) At that point, Dahlia returned to the arena floor, to stand with the rows of other challengers. Many couldn't attend because of their injuries. Aaresh was the only one who wasn't injured but had chosen to go home early regardless. She felt lonesome, knowing that he hadn't even wanted to finish one day in her company.

When Dahlia wasn't granted either third or second place, she was growing more and more anxious.

And then they called her name and that of Aeresh Raj.

The announcer had already been informed that Aaresh Raj had left for the day; the Elf explained to the audience that Dahlia Moon would be accepting the medal for her partner.

She wished he could've been there to share it with her. It felt wrong to go up to the stand and bask in the applause from the crowd all by herself. She knew that to the crowd, it probably seemed as though she were the one who had done most of the fighting, or at least the most evading. But she knew the truth. Aaresh's act of courage had been simply to accept her invitation on the spot, despite having no reason to help her at such a risk to himself when he clearly wasn't a fighter by nature.

He must've known right from the start that he wouldn't last long against a Dragon and a Slayer. And yet even when he understood what was involved, he stood by her side.

She couldn't have done it without him.

Ten

September 12
Sunrise: 06:46
Sunset: 19:19
Moon: Full Moon +1
Daylight: 12:32 hours

THE FOLLOWING MONDAY, Dahlia was invited back to Dragon Mountain. The apparatus for the street fair had been dismantled. There are no more booths on the long drive up to the Dragon caves. Even the caves themselves were closed today to tourists. But two Dragons in human form, wearing suits and badges, escorted her through a series of furnished hallways and chambers until she came to an elegant receiving room. The Emperor and Empress, also in human form, and also in formal business attire, waited there, along with a third woman, who was almost as short as Dahlia, and who, even in human form, showed two cat ears.

Dahlia had controlled her excitement up to now, but faced with three Guardians in a private setting, her heart started racing and her mouth dried like autumn leaves.

"Welcome, Dahlia Moon," said the Empress. "I'm Victoria Long, this is my husband, Troy Stern, and this is Moxie Bridgestone."

The small, clinical part of Dahlia's mind observed that Empress Victoria did not use any of their titles, and also that Victoria hadn't changed her last name upon her marriage. These dry reflections helped Dahlia focus her mind, remember she was a professional, and find her tongue. The Empress had not used titles, but that didn't mean Dahlia had to be rude.

She bowed formally. "*Sarmateem*," she said, using the ancient word for 'Guardians.' "It is an honor to meet all of you."

"Please be seated, and feel at ease," said Victoria. "We wish to have a frank discussion."

A formal tea set and assorted delicacies had already been spread on the table in the receiving room. Victoria silently and expertly served the tea. After the ceremony and the pleasantries, Victoria broached the real topic of the meeting.

"I understand that you are interested in doing prisoner recovery work," Victoria said.

"We were impressed with your fighting skills," said Troy. Up close, he still retained an aura of power and charisma. Yet his demeanor was unpretentious and friendly, as if he were a golden knight who had stepped out of a fairy-tale, then moved in next door to pass as an ordinary guy. "But we would like to emphasize that this assignment is for you alone, not your partner. He was a brave man, but currently we are looking for someone who can use stealth and discretion. Will that be an issue?"

"We were only partners for the contest," said Dahlia. "He has no interest in Bounty Hunting as a career."

"We believe your talents will be uniquely suited to bringing in the Person of Interest," said Victoria. "The Person in question is not exactly a criminal. In fact, he is Moxie's brother."

Dahlia blinked at the cat-eared Guardian of Strength, Moxie Bridgestone, in surprise. Moxie's ears laid back against her head, matching the anxiety on her face.

"He and I were prisoners together," said Moxie. "I went back to free him, and I succeeded, but we were separated in the escape. Now I don't know what's happened to him. I don't know if he's a prisoner again, or if he is simply living incognito."

"Unfortunately," said Victoria, with a sorrowful glance at Moxie, "The truth is that he may be dangerous."

"One of the human scientists who was last seen with my brother was recently found dead—mauled to death," said Moxie.

"Does your brother have a name?" asked Dahlia.

"They labeled him Specimen Number 219. Privately, the two of us chose our own names, but I don't know if he's using the names we chose. He picked 'Arash,' which means Archer of Light, and we've investigated anyone with that name. Within a hundred mile radius, there are eleven arcanes with that name, or some variation, including the Centaur who entered the contest with you, who works at Arcana Academy. But there are no Lion Shifters."

"We assume he either changed his name or got the heck of out of Dodge," said Troy.

"That sounds like a better assumption. Wouldn't he

have wanted to get as far from Arcana Glen as possible?" asked Dahlia.

"Maybe not," said Moxie. "He might have stayed because I'm here. Just because he hasn't contacted me yet doesn't mean he isn't planning to."

Troy cleared his throat. "Not to understate his brotherly affection, but he may also have stayed nearby because we have the richest leylines of Elemental magic in this part of the world. If he didn't want to leave the country, but wanted easy access to Elemental magic, he might have stayed."

"So he has magic as well," said Dahlia.

"Oh, yes. Probably Elemental Fire."

"He may wish to come in or he may resist," continued Victoria. "We simply have no way of knowing. We don't want him hurt. But we want someone who can use lethal force if no other option is on the table."

Lethal force. Dahlia's stomach tightened.

Moxie sat stiffly, but she nodded once. For some reason, Moxie was okay with this. But Dahlia wasn't sure *she* was okay with it.

Nonetheless, Dahlia inclined her head and answered diplomatically. "It would be a great honor to serve you in any way I can."

Emperor Troy gravely handed Dahlia a thick paper file. It was similar to a file she might receive for a bounty, but instead of a police report and a mug shot, there seem to be some kind of other bureaucratic records that she did not recognize. The word in the header of the documents was an acronym: KADABRA.

The records included a long list of horrific experiments that belonged in a horror movie and not in anyone's biography. There was no picture of a man in human form, but there was a photograph of a huge Lion Shifter. To provide a sense of scale, a human body, badly mutilated, lay on the floor in front of the Lion—apparently mauled to death by the Lion. The size of the beast was unreal. The Lion was obviously magical, yet there were implants in his fur, some kind of horrific technological interface. The Lion was also collared with a spiked, electronic harness. The label on the harness also read: KADABRA.

"I thought this place was only a myth," said Dahlia slowly. "You mean there really is a secret laboratory in the mountains right around our town, where humans experiment on arcanes? Especially on Shifters?"

"That is correct."

Anger welled up inside of her. "And you—you Guardians—you allow this? Why haven't you put an end to it?"

Troy huffed an angry breath. But he wasn't angry at Dahlia. "For the good reason that up until now they have held the threat of unleashing a doomsday weapon if we make any moves against them directly. Such a weapon threatens not only arcanes, but all mortals on the Mundane Sphere. While we might be willing to risk our own destruction, we have no right to decide that for those who live in ignorance of the threat." He remained calm yet brimmed with suppressed fury. "We have agents inside the base and the laboratory who have told us that recently the doomsday weapon was stolen. Or moved. It is not clear which. It is still in Arcana Glen, apparently taken by this Person."

He tapped the file of the Lion Shifter.

"What we don't know is if he took it to deny KADABRA use of the weapon, or if he is still working for them, willingly or unwillingly. It is possible he and the weapon were both moved together to hide the doomsday weapon from us because they found out that we know about it.”

“Why would a Shifter work for humans who have done this to him?” Dahlia looked at Moxie.

The other two Guardians also waited for Moxie to answer.

Moxie squirmed and pinched her hands together. “One, because he was traumatized, tortured into compliance, and brainwashed. Two, because he might have been told lies about who really funds and commands the so-called ‘human’ base. This entire base is actually run by the Court of Swords, from Winterdom, by the Azir. But maybe the Azir told him they’ve only recently taken over the base, and presented themselves as saviors of the Shifters, fellow arcanes fighting together against humans. We don’t know.”

“The Azir truly have a foothold here on the Mundane Sphere?”

“They absolutely do. But they are planning to expand that. They wish to conquer this Sphere as they have already conquered the Elven Spheres. We know they are building a tower here in Mundania which is meant to somehow connect all the Spheres together. We believe that we’re close to finding the new Guardian of the Tower, and he can help us destroy the Tower before the enemy can implement their plan. But, again, if we make any move to destroy the Tower while the doomsday weapon is still out there, we risk the enemy deploying the weapon in revenge. If they can’t win, they’ll take everyone out with them. So we *must* recover the weapon first.”

“But aren’t they losing the war, at last?” Dahlia said. “We fought in the arena in the capital of the Elvish kingdom in Autumndelle. Autumndelle and Springville have been liberated!”

"Only partially. The Winter Elves believe, with good reason, that if they were to conquer Mundania, they could retake the territory they have lost in the last year. Of course, this would involve slaughtering the Guardians a second time. In order to do that, they would detonate their magical doomsday weapon that would take out most of the continent of North America and render much of the human world uninhabitable to any but their own kind. Some arcanes would survive. If they detonate the weapon, the results would be worse than if the humans had a nuclear war. The entire surface of the planet would be irradiated and poisoned. Ten thousand years of winter would follow. Obviously, the Winter Elves could still survive in such an environment, along with their allies, the Ice Giants and whichever Witch and Shifter slaves they choose to keep alive.

"You can see," Troy concluded grimly, "Why we would prefer to avoid that scenario."

"We want you to save the Lion, not hurt him," said Victoria. "And not just because he is the brother of one of the Guardians whom we all love dearly." She nodded at Moxie. "But because we have every reason to believe this Lion Shifter is a good person, a victim of the war mongers, not a willing participant. But..." Victoria spread her hands.

"I'm certain my brother is not still working for KADABRA, but..." Moxie stared at her lap.

"We want certainty," said Troy, "but we can't afford to make a mistake. We can't afford to let the doomsday weapon be detonated, from either ignorance or malice."

All three awaited a response, but what could Dahlia say?

"I understand, *Sarmateem*," she said. "The priority is to retrieve the doomsday weapon, and if possible, also the

Person of Interest, but the Person of Interest must not be allowed to interfere with the primary mission."

They both nodded.

"The doomsday weapon is very small, only slightly larger than an ostrich egg," said Troy. "Which is not surprising, because it was originally made from an egg. We call it the Phoenix Egg, though it's not an egg inside anymore. It is deep red with gold patterns over the shell. The shell is made out of a hard metallic material, so a human would easily mistake it for a work of art or a mechanical device. But originally, it was magically fabricated out of an actual egg from a genetically altered Phoenix. The scientists of the laboratory, funded and directed so by the Court of Swords, have turned what was once a living egg into a destructive bomb. It uses both magic and earthly physics to create the equivalent of a fusion reaction along with a curse. The only way to ensure the weapon is destroyed is to detonate it within a magical shield, and even then, the explosion must safely underground."

"If I find this Phoenix Egg, how can I safely carry it in order to dispose of it?" asked Dahlia. "Can I simply banish it to the void?"

"We suspect that any attempt to remove the Phoenix Egg would result in instantaneous detonation," said Troy. "So you have to destroy it here, in the Mundane Sphere. We will give you a spell that will safely contain the explosion and show you how to access a shaft that leads to a pocket in the mantle of the earth. Only that is far enough underground that the Phoenix Egg can be destroyed without taking out the rest of the planet.

"We will also give you a way to find the phoenix's egg," said the Empress. "Come with us. We are going to give you some tools that would make Batman and James Bond drool."

~

Empress Victoria and Emperor Troy took Dahlia into another cavern that had been turned into a living space. This room was less finished than the other; Dahlia could still see spots of raw rock in the walls and ceiling. However, the floor of the room was lined with tables and cabinets that held every imaginable sort of weapon and device. She knew this was only a small portion of the fabled dragon horde of treasure. In addition to their level of jewels and gold, dragons also like to collect weapons and magical amulets of every sort.

They gave her a crossbow that was small enough to easily fit her hands. It was as easy to fire as a gun. And it was as powerful as a gun, with a range over a mile, according to the Emperor, who added, "But it shoots bolts instead of bullets. The bolts will put any being to sleep in a matter of seconds, no matter how large or powerful or magical. We want to emphasize that if we can bring the Lion in alive, that is preferred."

"We only want you to kill him if there's no other way to safely retrieve intact the Phoenix Egg," added the Empress.

"The bow is more than a weapon," said the Emperor. "You can see it has a compass built into it. This compass can be detached or can be left on the weapon. The compass will guide you directly to the Phoenix Egg. It will always point in the direction of the egg rather than due North."

He showed her how the compass could be detached and worn as a medallion on a necklace or left fastened to the bow. When left attached to the crossbow, the crossbow would physically rotate toward the target, not just the compass itself, but the actual point of the bolt fixed into the weapon. Unlike a traditional bow and arrow, she could leave a bolt ready to go without maintaining tension on a string.

Both of the objects, the compass and the crossbow, were beautifully embossed works of art, in addition to being practical tools. She saw the alchemical symbol for Stone engraved into the exotic metals of the crossbow and realized it had been made with Elemental Stone magic. The compass had the alchemical symbols for Wind; obviously it had been crafted with Elemental Wind magic.

Therefore, she wasn't surprised when the final two objects given to her were engraved with the symbols of Water and Fire.

The object that used Elemental Water was a small beautifully engraved flask. It looked large enough to contain only a cup or two of real water, but the Guardians explained that it would pour out as much liquid as she needed to create a circle around her target.

"This Elemental Water will create a shield. We know that you have Elemental Water magic, so you will be able to use your own magic to reinforce this shield, but use this as a foundation, and it will augment your power. You can create a huge sphere, with a hemisphere above ground level and the other hemisphere below, so that nothing can get in and out from any of the six cardinal directions: North, East, South, West, Above or Below.

"The Fire device, on the other hand, is very simple."

They showed it to her. It was disguised as an ordinary lighter, again very beautifully embossed.

"This is not a lighter, please don't try to help someone light up a cigarette with it. It will latch onto the Phoenix

Egg when brought into contact with it. The device will seal onto the egg. After that, it will be primed to detonate the egg. The trigger button is exactly the way you would turn on a lighter. Keep this device in the ether until you need it, so no one can steal it from you, nor can you drop it accidentally during combat or when you change your clothes. You do know how to store things in the ether, don't you?"

She nodded.

She felt humbled, almost terrified, by the opportunity offered to her. She had hoped for an opportunity to prove herself, but this mission was much bigger than her career as a bounty hunter. She might even lose her life in this mission.

It was no longer a question of taking a risk just because she did not want to be a cook in her parents' restaurant. The very lives of her family and the future of all the generations of everyone on Earth could depend on her failure or success.

It was overwhelming. It also gave her even more determination to succeed.

The Empress and Emperor gave her their formal blessing to begin her hunt.

Eleven

September 16
Sunrise: 06:50
Sunset: 19:12
Moon: Waning Gibbous
Daylight: 12:22 hours

AARESH LOVED WORKING at a job where his workday was over at three in the afternoon. That gave him plenty of time to get home before sunset. He had been embarrassed to reveal to Dahlia that as a grown man he was scared of the dark, but his fear of subterranean structures, as well as his urgency to get home before sundown, had been no joke. Bad things happened in secret dark underground facilities, and bad things happen after sunset. He preferred to be safe inside the house he had bought, refurbished, and turned into both a sanctuary and a fortress.

However, as a lion he had a huge appetite and that meant huge grocery expeditions. He found that none of the local stores had food for him, so on Friday after school, he drove his special gold van to a larger town to go to one of the big wholesale stores and buy bulk amounts of meat, greens, dairy products, fruits and vegetables. And more meat. By the time he returned to the winding roads of Arcana Glen, headed towards his mansion hidden on a secluded mountainside, it was almost sunset.

A Hummer with tinted windows had been following him home ever since he entered the outskirts of Arcana Glen. As long as he was on the main roads, he could explain away the car's presence as a coincidence, but when he turned up the twisty mountain road that serviced only a few remote houses on the hillside, his suspicions, already on a hair trigger, rose to paranoia levels.

Someone has been watching for a shopper who buys large amounts of meat, he thought. Their team followed me from the store. They want to know where I live.

One of his paramount rules was that no one knew where he lived. No one. Not even the school where he worked had his real address. He used a PO Box in a nearby town.

Rather than lead whoever was following him back to his house, Aaresh pulled off on another small road that he knew led to the house of a dissolute billionaire playboy. Then he drove into the woods and parked the car behind the trees. His oversized van was especially altered and designed so that he could drive it even in his lion form. To other arcanes, it would look like he had adjusted it to drive as a centaur; odd, but doable, since they would see him with human arms operating the steering wheel, standing in a big service van with the seats removed. To humans, of course, he would just look like a normal man behind the wheel of a very tall, tough old van.

No one would see the true and extremely absurd sight of a giant lion operating a steering wheel that was like a toy between his huge golden paws.

I would make a great character in a children's television show, he often thought when climbing into his car. Even though it was oversized compared to most vehicles on the road, a monster car, he was still cramped. It felt good to climb out of the car and pad softly through the woods. He sniffed the air.

Sure enough, his stalkers drove up the same dirt road he had taken and parked their own vehicle not far away. There were five of them. He sniffed again, locating them. Then he saw them creeping through the forest behind him.

White Wolves. They had snow white hair, even pale eyebrows and pale skin in their human form. They all wore silver-studded collars. Slaves themselves, they would still serve their masters faithfully. These hunters worked for the Azir—the Winter Elves.

Aaresh suppressed a growl that gathered deep in his throat. He knew those collars. They have been designed by the laboratory that made him. He had worn one, once.

That was the strangest thing about KADABRA. Most of the humans who worked there hated arcanes; they regarded Shifters as mindless animals and Elves as indistinguishable from demons. They were clueless that the power behind their entire organization was, ironically, the Azir Court of Swords—and their allies from Darkpyre—literal demons. It reminded Aaresh of the warning from Nietzsche, that those who stare too long into the abyss found the abyss staring back. Humans had become the monsters they thought they were freeing the world from.

The White Wolves moved like a pack. They spoke confidently. They sniffed the air, as Aaresh had.

Indeed, as he watched from his place in the tall evergreen he had climbed just as easily as any house cat, the five White Wolves transformed simultaneously into their animal form. The White Wolves were very beautiful in their own wild and cruel way. Like him, they were much bigger than the natural animal that lived on earth. They were as large as horses. Still small compared to him, but with jaws and claws that could take out most other creatures with one bite or swipe.

He could easily defeat any one of them one on one, but a match of five against one might be a different story. The main reason he wanted to avoid a confrontation, however, was that he had no wish to kill them. Although he was certain they were loyal to their evil masters, he pitied them. Likely they had been born into slavery and knew of no other life. He could sympathize with that.

The White Wolves surrounded his car, sniffing it and getting his scent. Damn. Unless he killed them, he would have no way of preventing them from memorizing his scent and picking up his trail in the future if they came across him anywhere. Aaresh did not wish to kill them, but how could he stop these hounds from finding him again if he did not?

~

September 16
Sunrise: 06:50
Sunset: 19:12
Moon: Waning Gibbous
Daylight: 12:22 hours

The Emperor and Empress had asked Dahlia to be discreet. She was not to openly change her routine during her hunt. She kept teaching classes, and made a show of being seen at her family's restaurant, Bao & Bun during the day—from time to time.

But secretly, every day and every night, she devoted hours to the hunt.

Despite the powerful tools she'd been given, it wasn't easy. Nothing should have been able to shield the Doomsday Weapon from the magic compass, yet the readings were erratic and unreliable. Something was interfering, but what? A shield spell? A chaos spell? Hiding the device in the ether?

The only problem was that doing any of those things to the Doomsday Weapon risked setting it off. Surely the Lion who had stolen it *knew* that? Or was he really willing to risk destroying the Earth to hide his location?

The compass and crossbow pointed Dahlia in the direction she needed to go, so she started simply following that direction in a straight line as well as she could. In a mountain town like Arcana Glen, however, walking in any direction in a straight line was not that simple. Not only that, but to her confusion, the compass sometimes moved for no apparent reason into a different direction.

Whoever has the Phoenix Egg is not keeping it in one place, she realized. It's mobile.

What could that mean? Either they happened to be moving it every time she started tracking it, or they moved it frequently to avoid anyone doing exactly what she was doing, using a spell to find it. Or someone was driving it around or carrying it in a suitcase or a container.

The Phoenix Egg was too large to wear as personal adornment or hide in one's pocket. But it was small enough that it could be put into a satchel or a briefcase or a box. The Phoenix Egg could not be stored in the ether without destroying the delicate spells around it. It had to be kept in the physical world. That was her only advantage and was related to the message the Guardians said was used to create the trucking spell in the first place. They hadn't explained the details of how that worked, and she doubted she would've understood even if they had. She was simply glad that her target, even if it was moved by someone, could not be moved through a portal where her tracking spell could not follow.

The Emperor and Empress had said there was no reason that the enemy had to store the Phoenix Egg close to Arcana Glen in order to threaten the Guardians. The explosive device would cause so much destruction that it could be kept anywhere in the northern hemisphere and still kill all the Guardians, and still kill most of life on earth. And yet, based on how the arrow moved, Dahlia had a sense that it was still in Arcana Glen.

In her bunny form she could move quickly. When the compass found a bead, she raced forward up the mountain and through the trees in that direction. Then she switched back to human form to check her compass to make sure it had not changed again, and then darted forward. Because the Phoenix Egg target was moving, she had to sometimes reorient herself and backtrack. It was impossible to tell if she was making real progress or simply hopping in circles.

And then she found wolf tracks.

There were five large wolves moving together. From the military formation of the wolves, which denoted human level intelligence, Dahlia knew they were Shifters. She would've known that from the size of the paws in any case, but this was not some gang of teenagers out for a howl.

These were large, militarily trained, experienced shapeshifting Hunters.

And it looked like they were after the same thing she was.

This was not entirely unexpected. The Guardians had warned her that the laboratory of KADABRA might send out teams to recover the Doomsday Device and the Lion. It might be one team, or they might be separate teams, it was hard to say. Either way, they would not be friendly to Dahlia, even if they seemed to be hunting the same thing. If they captured her, she could find herself facing a fate worse than death: imprisonment, experimentation, vivisection or enslavement.

Given that she was hunting Wolves, and given that they would gladly turn over a fellow Shifter to their evil ministers, did she dare take her bunny form?

There was no question; as dangerous as that might be to her, she wasn't fast enough as a human. She switched to her alter form and used her sensitive nose to follow the tracks. Every instinct of her rabbit told her to do the opposite, to run from predators, not to follow them. But she had good human cognition even in her animal form and overrode her fears.

She smelled blood. Had they killed the lion?

She switched back to human form, still running through the snow. There, smashed up against the tree, as if he had been thrown by a great force, was the bloody body of a White Wolf, twisted and mangled. Blood, still vivid and fresh, reddened his white fur.

She backed away from the corpse, but it was too late. Four other Wolves emerged at points all around her. Their eyes gleamed gold. They sniffed their fallen comrade and broke into angry howls.

They couldn't speak in their animal form, but she could tell from their offensive and angry postures that they thought Dahlia had killed their fellow wolf.

The Wolfpack pounced on her from all directions at once and she dropped again into bunny form and ran like hell.

Twelve

September 16
Sunrise: 06:50
Sunset: 19:12
Moon: Waning Gibbous
Daylight: 12:22 hours

DAHLIA WANTED to lead the Wolves away from the trail that she needed to follow. It was hard to resist using her cloaking magic, but she deliberately remained visible. The temptation to invoke her spell and make herself not only invisible but untraceable in every way was overwhelming. Water was truly an amazing element. It could catch the light and tick the eye. It could capture pheromones and spread them, but it could also dilute them down and mix them with other smells, confusing the nose. Water could sound as loud as thunder when poured in great amounts, but it could also muffle sound like a blanket of snow and confuse the ear. Water could wash away any footprints.

She had to resist that temptation.

She could escape wolves. Even these trained hunters. But before she became invisible, she had to make sure she didn't cross paths with them again. If they were hunting the same thing she was, she had to be the distraction that threw them off the trail.

The only problem was that they were faster than any Wolves she had encountered before, and they might run her to the ground before she was able to lead them far enough away.

One of the four Wolves took a shortcut, leaped in front of her, and enabled the other three Wolves to catch up and surround her again. Dahlia wondered if she needed to switch to invisible, when suddenly a new element entered the picture.

A human ran into the middle of the wolfpack and tackled one of the wolves without any hesitation. Even though he wasn't wearing any clothes and was much smaller and lighter compared to the Wolf Shifter, the man wrestled the beast as if he had done so all his life. For a human, he was *strong*. He was also buck naked.

It was her friend "Tarzan" from earlier. Gloriously naked and muscular, like some Neanderthal out of prehistory, some Wild Man raised by wild apes, he took on all four giant Wolves without any hesitation. He tossed them through the air like puppies. Finally, although none had died yet, they realized that he was too much for them. Whimpering and limping on injured paws, they ran away from a single naked human man.

And then the Wild Man turned his eyes on Dahlia.

～

He was so savage and strange that she wasn't certain she could evade him as a rabbit. As before, bunny's reaction to the Wild Man was incoherent attraction. The idiot rabbit wanted to go towards him. She refused to run.

Maybe if Dahlia faced him as a human woman, he would stop growling like a beast and talk to her. Like a civilized human being. It hadn't worked before, but Dahlia didn't know what else to do. She switched to her human form. Her clothing came with her shift, so she, at least, was dressed.

"Who are you?" Dahlia demanded. "Are you trying to save me? Or are you just enemies of those wolves?"

An inarticulate yelp came from his throat, like a bark or cry. It wasn't an animal's sound, but it definitely wasn't speech. She could imagine Neanderthals making grunts like that as they knapped stones over a fire stolen from a rival tribe.

Dahlia backed away. The Wild Man advanced. She realized that he was going to try to take her. She couldn't sense predatory intentions from his mind the way she had from the wolfpack but she now knew that was only because her empathy was looking for intentional *hunting thoughts*, not just the raw instinct of an animal. Real animals were no threat to her, so she had trained herself to be aware of the most dangerous hunters of all: those with human level intelligence.

She could no more sense the Wild Man's mind than she could that of a cougar or wolverine.

The Wild Man lurched forward, and he was so dang fast that even though Dahlia shifted to a rabbit, he caught her in his arms. Afraid of being strangled or bashed against a rock like a meal, she switched back to human form, but it didn't seem to matter to him which form she was in. He slung her over his shoulder like a caveman dragging his mate—or his meat?—home.

He was incredibly strong. She had never met a human as strong as this. There was no way for her to wiggle free. He carried her through the woods as if he had a goal in mind. The air grew thin and cold. The night deepened as he climbed higher up the mountain slope. Finally, he brought her to a natural cave.

These mountains were all riddled with caverns. The ones the Dragons used were huge and filled with beautiful rock formations from thousands of years of geological processes that exposed limestone and crystal.

This cave was not like that. It was just a cavity in the side of the mountain, claustrophobic and dark. From the stench, Dahlia guessed that a mountain lion, a mundane animal, not a Shifter, had once used it as a den. The smell was very old though; the Wild Man smell of her barbarian captor was much fresher.

She found out what had happened to the previous tenant of the cave when he threw her down on the skin of a lion. It had not been tanned and had dried into a stiff rather than soft mat on the stone floor. Still, it was the closest he had to any kind of furnishing in his cave.

"I've heard of man caves," she muttered, "but this is ridiculous."

After he lowered her onto the lion fur, the Wild Man squatted in front of her. He didn't need any words to explain to her the desire in his eyes or the arousal evident from his naked body.

The Wild Man wanted to mate with her.

Shifters could be notoriously animalistic about choosing their mates. Instinct, something to do with both scent and magic, gave some Shifters an instantaneous recognition of their mate. It didn't work as well in Bunny Shifters, with their notorious optimism toward mating, but even for them, if they found a true lifemate, the bond would hold, and they would be monogamous. Dahlia had heard stories of Shifters who met their life mate and immediately tore each other's clothes off and boinked like animals. In human form, but with primal, raw passion.

But who was this Wild Man? Was he shifter or human? Or something else? He wanted her, but was it a magical bond that he sensed or just an animalistic need to rut?

It doesn't matter, she reminded herself, because she wasn't going to rut with him *or* mate with him. She was going to escape.

The Wild Man had other ideas.

He shadowed her body with his after he set her on the rug. His hands, large and warm, traced the lines of her body. With gentle but irresistible motions, he positioned her on the lion fur, arranging her on her hands and knees. His hot, delicious breath tingled against the back of her neck. Unconsciously, she arched her back and thrust out her hips. He drew in a sharp breath.

Then he positioned himself behind her.

Oh, Light! She gasped. He had the brilliant idea he was going to mount her from behind. And her bunny was ready for it, lifting her hips up for him...

No! she chastised her bunny. I am not having wild doggy-style sex in a cave with a Wild Man!

When Dahlia squirmed away and tried to escape the cave, the Wild Man grinned at her. He took it as some kind of foreplay. He stalked her again, pounced on her when she tried to run, then tossed her back onto the lion skin and once again tried to make her assume the position on all fours.

This time she scampered away and backed into the cave.

"No!" she shouted. "I am not going to. I don't want it, do you understand? No!"

She really didn't expect that to work on someone who didn't understand human language and obviously had no concept of civilization or consent.

But he withdrew from her, sitting again in a squatting position. This time his eyes looked confused and hurt. But he didn't try to approach her again.

He also still would not let her leave the cave. He squatted there all night. She tried talking to him in different languages. She knew English and Korean, some Spanish and some French. He not only did not recognize any of them, he didn't seem to recognize language as such. All he did in return was grunt at her.

She even tried saying, as she tapped her chest, "Me Dahlia, you...?"

But when she gestured to herself, then him, he apparently thought she was trying to have sex with him and grabbed her again. She had to start the whole pushing and shouting "No!" all over again. She decided she wasn't going to touch him.

"Me Dahlia, you Tarzan," was still too civilized for him.

A few more times during the night, the Wild Man crawled towards her, sniffed her hair and once again tried to mount her, and she once again pushed him away. He was obviously stronger than she was, and could have overpowered her, but he accepted her rejections with a great deal of hurt. He stared at her like a puppy that had been yelled at for trying to snatch food from the table. *Why are you doing this to me?* he seemed to ask her morosely. *All I want is to make you happy. And eat you.*

Oh, no, she shouldn't have thought about that. Suddenly she had a very naughty image of him...

Hot embarrassment flamed her cheeks. There was something very tempting about the raw sexuality of the Wild Man. She had a feeling if she allowed herself to give in, it would be the most primal, most passionate, raw and delicious sex of her life. But...

Then what? She wasn't going to live the rest of her life in a cave sleeping on a stiff, smelly lion fur.

She tried to engage him in conversation and became more and more frustrated when he could not reply in kind. But he was just as frustrated that she wouldn't reply in kind to his simple basic sexual overtures.

"This just takes the classic male-female differences to a whole new level," she said sarcastically. "But you can't even appreciate the humor in it can you, my Tarzan friend?"

Finally, too exhausted to stay awake any longer and finally trusting enough that he would not force her against her will despite his barbarism, she fell asleep on the stinking lion skin.

Thirteen

September 17
Sunrise: 06:51
Sunset: 19:11
Moon: Last Quarter
Daylight: 12:19 hours

DAHLIA WOKE up in a beautiful bed in a gorgeously furnished room. The first thing she was aware of was how smooth and clean the sheets were. The thread count must be over 800 she thought, feeling the expanse of cool silk on either side of her. The super king-sized bed was a four-poster masterpiece, but the embroidered curtains had been pulled back so that she could see the sunlight pouring through huge French windows at the far end of the room.

All of the tints and shades in the room were gold, navy, butter yellow or sky blue; the room had a distinctly masculine flavor. It was large enough to be a bedroom, office and living room all in one, so in addition to the super-sized bed, there was a set of dark blue couches and reclining chairs tooled with metal gold sunburst patterns that matched the gold sunburst on the navy duvet on the bed, sheets, and curtains.

A gaming chair was positioned in front of a huge flat screen with several different game consoles and a shelf with a huge selection of video games. A pool table, dark blue instead of green, also fit easily in the room, as did a small private gym. Even the leather seating on the exercise equipment was blue with metallic gold sunburst patterns.

Finally, there was a small refrigerator and bar in the room. The bottles were a selection of blue and gold, and the bar almost looked more decorative than useful.

Now this was one mighty fine man cave. Much improved over a lion skin in a crevice in the rock. But how had she gotten here? She glanced down at her body and was embarrassed to find she had been bandaged and washed and left between the sheets entirely naked.

Disturbing. Who had stripped her? The caveman or the civilized owner of this gorgeous room?

Thank goodness she had stored a number of useful things in the ether before she started this hunt. She snapped her fingers and procured one of the extra outfits she packed. Wearing sensible pants and a T-shirt, and once again armed with an ordinary tranquilizer gun, she climbed out of bed. She did not bring the magical compass or crossbow out of the ether yet because she did not know if someone was watching her, perhaps through magic or perhaps through secret cameras. She needed to know more about who had rescued her—or captured her—and what they wanted from her.

～

The house was unlike any other she had ever visited. Two curving stories wrapped in a circle around a central courtyard, containing a round swimming pool and a barbeque area. The tiles on the bottom of the pool matched the sun patterns in the bedroom. The design of the mansion itself was classical Grecian, all white marble, and elegant pillars. The second story had a balcony all around the inner ring, overlooking the courtyard.

Around the balcony, there were ten doors in all, one of which led back to the bedroom. Dahlia circled the balcony, examining the doors. Every doorway was itself a work of art, and with the exception of the bedroom door, painted with exquisite classical murals of one of the Nine Muses. The doors weren't locked.

She opened the first door, dedicated to Clio, the Muse of History, who was depicted with a clarion (a war trumpet) in one hand, and a book in the other. The door opened into a huge wedge-shaped room entirely given over to a library: floor to ceiling books, two stories high, with an open center and a catwalk that met up with the threshold where Dahlia stood. Down on the floor, more shelves were on some kind of metal rail, operated with a turnstile, so that they could be compressed together when not in use. Beyond that was a well-lit desk with a huge, strange stool before it. There were large pens and stacks of paper on the desk, but no computer.

Except for the bedroom, which was only one story high, placed above the atrium that led into the house, all of the other nine rooms were two-stories high. Each one was dedicated to the art of a different Muse. The next room after the library, that of Euterpe, was a music room, which held not only a grand piano at the center, but an orchestra's worth of other instruments. The chamber dedicated to Thalia, the

Muse of Comedy, held another library, but this library included many forms of modern and older media, such as CDs, videotapes and film reels, as well as what looked like paper screenplays. This room also had a home theater with a huge flatscreen television. The room overseen by Melpomene, the Muse of Tragedy, included a similar library, with a silver screen instead of a television. Terpichore was usually considered the Muse of Dance, but her chamber had been decorated as a dojo, and weapons of all sorts hung on the walls. Erato, the Muse of Poetry, and Polymnia, the Muse of Hymns and Mathematics, included more library shelves, presumably dedicated to their related subjects. There was no doubt that the room of Ourania was dedicated to Science; a telescope aimed through a skylight at the center of the room. This room also had several computers. The last room, that of Calliope, the elder Muse, was dedicated to the Visual Arts, including many gorgeous paintings and lifelike statues. However, this was not the only room with visual art. All of the rooms, in addition to their other contents, had been embellished by fine art related to the room's theme.

There was, apparently, no Muse of Cooking. Clearly, that was a lacuna on the Greeks' part. There was also no kitchen anywhere that Dahlia could find, unless one counted the pathetic bar kitchenette in the corner of the bedroom.

What a peculiar house. If not for the bedroom, she would have guessed it wasn't a house at all, but a museum.

Keeping himself concealed from his guest, Aaresh watched his guest explore his house. Ever since he had escaped the laboratory, he had been collecting things for his den, his sanctuary. When he found this house, like a strange Roman Villa dedicated to the god of the sun, Apollo, it called to him as if it had been made specifically for him.

Many of the statues in the library had originally been decorations intended for outdoors. He doubted they were original, but he enjoyed looking at the classic sculptures. Many of the other works of art were originals, things he squandered his fortune on. After a burst of shopping, he slowed down and started to become more discerning in what he purchased. He intended his collection to be built up over a long, long time.

Originally the house had more rooms dedicated to things like kitchen, bedroom, living room, but he had collapsed all those functions into his single master bedroom suite. The only extra space was the bath house. That was reached by a covered walkway at the back of the Villa, and it was almost as large as the Villa itself. He loved it. He liked the swimming pool in the central courtyard as well, not so much for swimming as for sitting next to and occasionally dipping into. But he loved the bathhouse even more. He loved to keep clean.

He knew his collections were far from complete, and he watched anxiously for any sign of criticism in the face of the woman walking through the rooms he had dedicated to each of the Nine Muses. Did she recognize the classical reference? Did she appreciate his mixture of antiques and popular cultural references? Did she think it was corny or stupid? Or nerdy and tiresome? Aaresh longed to share his reasoning with her and to hear what impression she had and what additions she might suggest to add to his collection in the future.

It hadn't occurred to him when he started the collection that he would ever want to share it with someone. In fact, he had started the project as a way to console himself for the fact he would always be alone in his life. Because he was hunted by some very evil people, and because of his condition, he knew he would never be able to find a mate, as other Shifters did.

But then he had found that the Savage had captured Dahlia. Had the Savage recognized her smell as the night teacher who shared a room with him? Was this Aaresh's fault, for learning her smell, getting it on his clothes by fighting alongside her, and interesting the Savage in her? It was pointless to explain to the Savage that he was a broken, useless thing, a danger to himself and others. The Savage cared only about his own needs.

Aaresh's greatest fear was that the Savage had hurt her when he took her back to the cave. Aaresh had no doubt that the Savage had tried to ravage her, and Aaresh was tortured by the desire to ask her, but what if talking about it only made it more painful for her? He couldn't bring himself to ask. He was relieved when he discovered she wasn't crying, bleeding, or injured.

The Savage had not taken off her clothes. Aaresh had done that, knowing there was no danger of him feeling any physical attraction to her when he was in his lion form. Oh, he could admire her beauty at an intellectual level, the perfection of the feminine incarnation, much as he admired his statues; but the pheromonal attraction, the physical desire, simply wasn't there, thank the Light.

And yet, like the Savage, Aaresh *did* covet her, in a purely intellectual way. He wanted to collect her. She was an emblem of Beauty, inside and out, and he wanted to keep her in his home forever, like a museum piece. He wouldn't. He understood that was extremely wrong. He of all people, knew what it was like to be caged and held against one's will. He would never ever do that to another person.

But he longed to have her stay of her own free will.

He longed for it so hard that he even considered asking her. And, of course, that was absurd. He would be asking her to share his double life, his secret, his desperate need to constantly hide who he really was. And when she found out the curse that plagued him, she might turn away in disgust and regret agreeing to stay with him, but by then he would not dare let her go.

He couldn't tell her of his secret if she were not willing to keep it. And he couldn't find out if she were willing to keep his secret without telling her.

He was trapped.

It felt like a nail being driven through his heart. He not only could never have a lover; he could never even have a friend. His loneliness was complete and total. Knowing that, it only made it worse to torture himself watching her in his home. The best thing would be to encourage her to leave as soon as possible.

Fourteen

September 17
Sunrise: 06:51
Sunset: 19:11
Moon: Last Quarter
Daylight: 12:19 hours

"I SEE THAT YOU ARE AWAKE," a deep cultured voice said formally. Dahlia did not recognize the man's voice. He sounded urbane and regal. "I regret that I cannot be with you in person at the moment. I found you in the company of a certain savage who lives in these woods, and I thought you might appreciate more sophisticated sleeping arrangements until you recovered from your injuries."

She stared up at the corner but the only thing there was a speaker and a video camera. "Am I a prisoner?"

"Certainly not." He sounded offended. "Unlike the savage who captured you, I am not a barbarian. However, I do value my privacy. Therefore, when you feel ready to leave, you may do so only if you agree to wear a blindfold which includes a spell of confusion, so that you will not be able to find your way back to this house again. If you agree to that you may leave anytime you wish."

"Why are you so antisocial?"

"Those are my conditions."

"Very well," she said. "I wish to leave now."

A blindfold appeared on a table in front of her.

"Put on the blindfold."

She waved her hand over it, feeling with her empathy magic for any negative energy or evil intent. She could sense Chaos in the aura around the blindfold, but that must be the heart of the confusion spell. Real evil did not radiate from the blindfold. Finally, she put it on. At once she could no longer tell what direction was which. She even felt a little dizzy, as if she weren't certain anymore what was up and down.

She began to stagger and spread her hands out to either side trying to steady herself, although the problem was inside her. The chaos spell was confusing her sense of balance.

When she tried to take a step, she stumbled. How was she going to find her way out of here? She couldn't even walk anymore with no sense of balance.

"Climb on," a voice instructed. "Hold on, ride my back, and I will lead you away from here safely."

And then her hand encountered soft fur.

Her breath caught in her throat when she recognized the smell of the animal: *lion*.

Her rabbit kicked in hard, making her heart yammer in her ears, making her legs itch to kick out and leap and run.

But the animal was standing right in front of her, quiet, not attacking or raging. Obviously, it had to be a Shifter in his animal form. Very likely it was the same man who had just been speaking to her over the intercom although she had no way to be sure.

The fur just went on and on and on. How big was this animal?

Trying to climb on was more like mountain climbing than mounting a horse. The only animal larger that she had ever encountered was a Dragon. The Lion was even larger than the Centaur form of her professor friend, the day teacher, Mr Raj.

Her fingers groped in the fur. It was incredibly soft, much softer than the horsehair of the Centaur, definitely softer than dragonscale. But beneath the fur, she could feel the muscles, huge, tense, powerful.

Her fingers curled in longer fur. It was a slightly different texture than the first kind, also soft, but more like hair. She could even wrap long tendrils of it around her hands. She had to resist the urge to pet. And there was so much of it, covering a huge head like a halo.

It's a mane, she realized. Of course, it was a mane; he was a lion. A male lion. A huge lion, exactly like the one she had been tasked to find. Dahlia willed her heartbeat to slow back to something approaching normal as she analyzed the significance of this. She was probably standing in the presence of one of the two targets she had been sent to find.

Should she simply ask him about the Doomsday Weapon?

Or was he demanding that she leave, blindfolded, under

the influence of a confusion spell, because he already knew that she had come here to look for the Phoenix Egg?

He claimed he valued his privacy. But maybe he was protecting the weapon. If she admitted she was looking for it, she might lose her only chance to find it. As much as she wanted to trust him, the deadly consequences of being wrong convinced her to keep her silence. She needed to find out more and she needed to find the weapon *first*, not beg him to give it to her and risk the chance that he would refuse and simply slay her.

Suddenly, the muscles of the lion bunched and expanded under her as he took off in a leap. She squealed and fell forward against his mane, gripping it much harder than she had intended to because it was her only alternative if she did not want to slide off. He broke into a four-legged gallop that was both like and yet utterly unlike the gallop of a horse.

She knew when they left the house and entered the courtyard. She sensed when they passed through the atrium of the house. She smelled flowers in a garden.

Sunflowers?

It was daylight outside, and she felt cool September sunshine pour down onto her shoulders and hair. She leaned forward over his body as he galloped through the trees. She could tell they were going quite fast by how quickly shade alternated with sunlight against her face. He galloped so fast that she wasn't sure if she would have been able to keep track of where they went, even if the confusion spell had not been put on her control of her sense of direction.

The ride was terrifying and exhilarating, made worse by the fact that she was blindfolded and had to trust him completely. And her trust could be a huge mistake.

If he had even a suspicion of what she was after, it was possible he would be opposed to her. He could be leading her out into the woods to dispose of her far away from his own house. That specific fear became part of the general fear she would fall off and die on the leaps he made into the air, or that she would hit her head on a tree when he raced under branches so closely that pine leaves brushed the top of her head.

However, the lion not only seemed to have a good sense of his own presence in the woods, but he appeared to know exactly how much space she needed. He never let her bonk her head against a tree, nor did he travel so fast that she fell off his back. The few times she felt herself sliding to one side or the other he shrugged his shoulders and twisted his torso in such a way as to re-center her, actively helping her keep her perch.

It was a subtle, thoughtful gesture, done in the midst of a mad race from the house. It made her appreciate both his intelligence and his kindness. She hoped dearly that he was not helping the Court of Swords to threaten to enslave or destroy the Earth.

She would hate to find herself his enemy. He would make a very formidable foe. But she also hoped that he was what he seemed: as kind and thoughtful as he was powerful and intellectual.

Fifteen

September 20
  Sunrise: 06:54
  Sunset: 19:04
  Moon: Waning Crescent
  Daylight: 12:12 hours

Monday, Aaresh returned to work, as usual. But he was still tormented by the idea that the Savage had hurt Dahlia when he had her alone in the cave. Was there any way to find out? Could he ask once he was safely under the mask of his glamour as an ordinary school teacher?

To make it seem natural—accidental, he had to wait another day, until Tuesday, when she taught her class in the evening. On Tuesday, Aaresh finished at three as always and he had no errands to run today. Unfortunately, Dahlia's classes started at seven, four minutes before sunset. He didn't dare stay out after dark. He liked to be home an hour before sunset. At least the daylight hours were still longer than the hours of darkness, which meant he still had the upper hand...

After the Autumn Equinox, that would change. His powers would be weaker... the powers of darkness and ignorance would be stronger. This would be Aaresh's first winter spent free, and he still wasn't certain he would be able to handle the darkness on his own, without the shackles of the laboratory to restrain him. For the first time, he would have to be his own jailer during the months when his magic waned.

But he would deal with that when he came to it.

Today, he decided to take the risk of staying out closer to sunset to try to speak to Dahlia. If Dahlia arrived exactly on time, or late, he could never have a chance to talk to her. He didn't want to end up in a conversation with her and have to interrupt it in order to rush home. However, his need to see her and verify she was unmolested overwhelmed his usual worries.

So he waited. Half past six, she arrived. Thank the Light she was the kind of teacher who liked to prepare her classroom before the students showed up!

She was surprised but pleased to see him. She gave no indication of recognizing him as the giant lion or anyone else.

She smiled and cried, "I have your medal!"

"My medal?" He asked blankly.

"Yes, we won our challenge against the Emperor and Empress. I had to receive yours in your absence, but I kept it for you. If I had known I would see you today, I would have... but unfortunately..."

"It's quite alright," he said hastily. "Just wanted to make sure you had no... injuries."

For a moment she frowned at him. Then her face

cleared. "You mean from the match in the stadium. Oh, I wasn't injured, but, in any case, I heal quickly, as I see you do as well. No harm done."

"So... You're good then."

"Yep."

"Okay. I just wanted to make sure." Aaresh adjusted his glasses on his nose trying desperately to think of something intelligent to say to her to prolong the conversation. Actually, what he needed to do was *end* the conversation and get home. But he felt like a planet in orbit around a star. He couldn't escape her attraction.

"Come in," she said. "I have to set up, but you don't have to leave right away."

He followed her in like a puppy. Aaresh glanced around the classroom, as if looking for clues about her subject matter, but of course all he saw were the posters he himself had put on the walls during the teacher orientation a week before the students arrived. Unless she also taught Western Literature... What a coincidence that would be!

"Would you like to stay and watch my class?" she asked. "It's adult education so it's probably a little bit different than what you're used to."

"I would love to but..." He glanced at his watch. How had it already gotten so late? He noticed some men headed toward the classroom, probably students of hers, and realized he had zero interest in meeting them. The last thing he wanted was to get dragged into another long conversation with them instead of with her.

Watching her teach was another matter. He dearly would have loved to stay and watch her class, no matter what it was. But he was getting more and more anxious about getting home.

"Perhaps some other time," he said, trying to soften his

refusal with a smile. "I'm glad that you're okay. Take care of yourself. The world can be a dangerous place."

She raised her eyebrows. "It can, can't it? Fortunately, there are good people in the world. Sometimes where we least expect to find them."

~

That was odd.

At first, Dahlia had thought Aaresh Raj had come to ask her about the contest, but he hardly seemed to care about the results. Then she assumed that he was going to ask her out on a date, and she experienced a burst of energy and excitement. She planned to accept.

When he started fiddling with his glasses and running his fingers through his sexy black hair, she realized he was feeling shy, and was not going to ask her out. It was almost all she could do to restrain herself from asking him instead.

But some stubborn part of her wanted *him* to do it. Dating was one area of her life when she still enjoyed the feeling of being pursued. It was the one kind of hide and seek where she could run away, hoping to be found.

Instead, Aaresh started looking at his watch and hurried away. She watched him go, feeling a pang of disappointment. She was surprised at her own reaction. She didn't usually go for the nerdy type, so why was she so eager for him to ask her out anyway? It was not likely to go anywhere.

Zachary, one of her students, sauntered up to her.

"Hey," he said, "Before everyone else gets here, there's something I wanted to ask you. Would you be interested in going out with me sometime? Maybe after class we can go to one of the bars and have a few drinks."

That was exactly what she had hoped that Aaresh would say, but Dahlia wasn't interested in Zachary, even though on the surface he seemed more her type. Not an asshole, but aggressively confident, hyper masculine and interested in the same field she was. Yet she felt nothing. She declined with some excuse about teacher/student relations. The excuse didn't really apply to night school, certainly not bounty hunting license school, but it would have to work. She walked inside to get ready for class.

Dahlia ended class early on the pretext of giving them a break. The truth was that she had hurried through the material so that she could start the hunt earlier in the evening tonight. Pulling all-nighters and trying to catch up during the day was her usual lifestyle, so that wasn't the problem.

The problem was that she sensed that her quarry, the Lion Shifter, went to ground during the night. It struck her as odd that she had not met him until after sunrise. As a lion, he probably had the impulse to settle down in a den somewhere, but if the beautiful library was not his den, then where did he spend most of his time?

Or perhaps he spent most of the night prowling his territory. How else could he have found out that the Savage had captured her and stashed her away in a crevice in the face of the mountain? It wasn't like that cave was very easy to find.

Sixteen

September 21
Sunrise: 06:55
Sunset: 19:04
Moon: Waning Crescent
Daylight: 12:09 hours

MAYBE SHE WAS JUMPING to conclusions. Maybe the Lion Shifter with the refined house had nothing to do with the giant Lion she was supposed to be hunting. It's not as though there were not other Lion Shifters in Arcana Glen. She had been given the files on several of them, along with her assignment, in case the Target attempted to contact another Lion Shifter. One was in the Enchanted Circus who worked with Moxie. There were others. Furthermore, magically speaking, the lion totem was almost as popular as the wolf totem. Just as different magical traditions, founded on different Elements, had been drawn to create their own versions of Wolf avatar—

the Werewolves of Autumndelle, the Lycans of Winterdom, the Shamen Wolfwalkers of Springvale, the rare, mystical Flame Wolves of Summerland—the same was true of Lions. There were ordinary Animal Lion Shifters; the Merlions of Springvale; the Lammasu, the Winged Lions of Winterdom; the Shishi, the Stone Lions of Autumndelle that Dahlia and Aaresh had seen proctoring the arena in Autumndelle; and the rare and powerful Shamash, the Sun Lions of Summerland; in short, there were Lion Shifters from each realm, each tapping into a different kind of Elemental magic. Most were rare. She had no idea how many lived in Arcana Glen, but...

Perhaps the recluse who lived in a fancy Roman Villa in the mountains was a *different* giant Lion Shifter. He might have nothing whatsoever to do with the escapee from a creepy human military base.

Dahlia pulled her crossbow out of the ether and began to hunt. There was only one way to find out.

The trail took her deep into mountain forest and upward toward the peaks. Around midnight she crossed a magical barrier, and suddenly, where from afar, she had seen only more forest, she abruptly came into view of a gorgeous house that gleamed white in the moonlight. The classic Greek pillars at regular intervals the villa were unmistakable. Just in case she was wondering if there were *two* reclusive Lion Shifters who built Greek-style round villas in the middle of the Colorado Rockies, she saw that there were sunflowers in the garden surrounding the villa.

There could not be two such exotic, highly shielded houses in the vicinity of Arcana Glen. She had returned to the house of her gentleman host, despite his efforts to prevent her from finding it again.

She knew he would not be pleased. Even she was not

pleased. After his kind hospitality, the last thing she wanted to do was hunt him down and initiate a confrontation that could edge into violence.

But then she imagined an explosion so large it could take out most of a continent and cause 10,000 years of winter to envelop the Earth. No matter what else, she had to stop that.

She checked the compass on the bow once more. Yes, the Phoenix Egg was directly in front of her. Unfortunately, she could not tell how far away it was. It could be ten feet away or a mile away.

She put the bow into the ether. She knew that the Lion Shifter had cameras on his property, and she didn't want him to see any of her weapons. Before she could locate the Egg, she had to determine if the Lion was at home.

Dahlia gathered her mist of invisibility about her and proceeded very cautiously. With any luck, the Lion had hidden the Phoenix Egg among his art relics. Perhaps he had simply bought it from another collector, with no idea of its true danger. No, that was not likely. This *had* to be the Lion who had escaped from the laboratory, which meant he had taken the Doomsday Weapon directly from the laboratory also.

Surely, he had to know what he had taken, didn't he? Or had he simply stolen a number of things, with no idea what was what, what was useful and what was dangerous? It occurred to her that it was remarkable that an escaped prisoner had the money to afford this mansion. Either he was still working with the people who had experimented on him, or he had stolen things and sold them to use as his own little nest egg.

If that's what he had done, she didn't blame him. Surely, the scum owed him that, and much more, for what they had done to him. But again, everything revolved around the question. Was the Lion a willing participant in the evil scheme or an innocent caught in the crossfire?

Instead of the crossbow, maybe she should've brought the fabled Sword of Truth with her. She could have simply cleared everything up by asking him to swear to his innocence. Of course, that assumed she could force a Lion the size of an African elephant to do anything. No, the Guardians had made it clear that Dahlia had been selected for this job because they were counting on her stealth. She understood that and wasn't offended by it. The important thing was to get the job done one way or another.

Previously when she had explored the house, it had been daylight. It looked more mysterious and even ominous in the moonlight. Room after room flowed from one arched doorway to another, each room filled with priceless antiques and books and television and film mysteriously preserved on gold plated discs.

The first thing she did was confirm that no one was in the mansion. She sniffed every room and determined that the last time the Target had been there was yesterday. There was another smell that was familiar, but she couldn't quite pinpoint it.

Still, it was good that the Lion was not home. If she could take the Phoenix Egg without alerting him or alarming him, she would return immediately to the Empress and Emperor. She would tell them that, as far as she could tell, the Lion was not bothering anyone, but leave it up to their discretion to deal with him.

Now that she had time to explore the house at a more

relaxed pace, she could see that his collection was probably still expanding. Many of the bookshelves she had taken to be already full were still empty when she walked around them. Many of the art pieces were not real after all, but copies. She knew that only because he had pinned helpful little notes to distinguish the ones which were replicas and which were originals. He also had notes about where real versions of the replicas could be found, and whether they were for sale, indicating that he perhaps intended to acquire them in the future.

She was seeing not a museum in its mature phase, but in its planning phase. This fit with what she knew of the history of laboratory Lion. If he had escaped, it had been only a few months ago. He would not have had time to completely settle in.

Why did he stay in Arcana Glynn anyway? That was the thing that bothered her the most. It seemed like the best evidence he was still working for his old tormentors. Surely if he had wanted a fresh start, he would've stayed as far away from Arcana Glen as possible. According to the Empress and Emperor, that is what Moxie had done until she came back for the specific reason of trying to free her brother.

Dahlia searched every room twice and half of the rooms three times before morning. She could not find any sign of the Phoenix Egg. When she checked with the compass, it confusingly sent her in circles around the house. She couldn't understand what was going on.

She thought of the confusion spell that the Lion had used on the blindfold he made her wear when he took her out of the house. What if he had placed a spell like that on the egg itself? The Guardians seemed to think it wasn't possible to cast extra spells on the egg, because it was already so completely infused with magic that any more interference could set it off. But maybe they were wrong or there was some other form of magic at play that they did not know about.

Dahlia decided to quit for today, because she did not want to be here when morning light came. Also, she was growing exhausted. She heard a clock ringing, though she was not sure what hour of the day it was marking. She switched to her other form and hopped to the roof.

That's when she saw the sexy Centaur teacher, Aeresh Raj from the dayshift at Arcana Academy trotting up the driveway. Dahlia was stunned. What were the chances that the Centaur knew the Lion? Especially considering how vigorous the Lion was about protecting his privacy? She worried that maybe the Centaur had followed her here, and was about to encounter a dangerous top predator because he was interested in her but had been too shy to ask her out on a date...

That made no sense.

Even supposing she wasn't just projecting her fantasy onto him, and Aaresh actually liked her and wanted to ask her out, why would he wait all night before following her? How did it make any sense that he was so shy he couldn't ask her on a date but so bold that he would follow her into a stranger's house?

But she couldn't figure out any connection between a schoolteacher and a dangerous escaped laboratory prisoner. The schoolteacher was a Centaur, so there was no way he was one of the scientists who worked for the human organization. Even if they were secretly funded by Elves, they didn't know that. The humans were all very prejudiced against arcanes of any sort. Or were the humans ignorant of the Centaur's true nature? Like most arcanes, Centaurs could assume full human form, and hide their odd features, like horse ears, with a glamour...

A glamour. At the exact moment the idea hit her...

The Centaur crossed the shield hiding the property from the forest. The glamour fell away from his body; Dahlia recognized the significance of the sparkle around him when it happened right in front of her, even though the glamour had been of such a high quality she had no suspicion up until that moment it even existed.

When the glamour fully dissolved into mist and wind, his true body was revealed.

Aaresh Raj was not just a high school teacher of western literature. He was a huge Golden Lion with a coal-black mane that flickered with the sparks of Elemental Fire. He was a Shamash, a Sun Lion.

She was so shocked that she returned to human form with the crossbow in her hands ready to fire. It was an instinctive, defensive reaction. Fortunately, he didn't look up and see her on the roof. As she tracked him, the compass tracked him as well. The arrow was pointed right at him.

Somehow, he was carrying the Phoenix Egg with him. Supposedly it couldn't be taken into the ether, so he must have it in a pocket or a satchel.

Perhaps that explained the other completely inexplicable and unusual thing about this Lion.

He was wearing clothes.

In general, when Shifters went to their animal form, they did not wear clothing. The full shifters who became a complete animal often tore their clothing in the process of shifting, but even if they took off their clothing first, as animals, they did not feel the same kind of embarrassment over nudity that they would in their human form. In fact, some shifters had less embarrassment over nudity in any form because they were used to it as animals.

Demi-shifters, such as the centaur she had thought he was, were more likely to wear clothing, at least over their human parts. The classic example were mermaids who wore bikini tops. Not all mermaids were so shy. Like Rabbit Shifters, mermaids had a certain reputation for lustiness. The point was, even they did not wear clothes over their tails.

Dahlia had never seen a Shifter in his animal form attempt to wear clothing. The Lion, however, was wearing a vest and tie over a nice dress shirt. The collar of the shirt was hidden by his mane; the cuffs of the sleeves ended just above his forepaws. He even had pants specifically tailored (how else?) to bunch loosely over his enormous hind legs, leaving a hole for his tail.

It looked absolutely ridiculous.

He should've been an extremely dignified and terrifying sight, but in that absurd outfit, he looked like...

Well, he looked like he was ready to go teach elementary school children exciting fairytales about a Gentleman Lion.

Was he trying to look harmless? Was he so ignorant of how the real world worked because he had been raised in a dungeon that he had no idea Animal Shifters did not dress like humans?!

It was so bizarre!

She switched back to rabbit form after stashing compass and Bow and Arrow in the ether. She had studied his house while she explored it and knew that there was a veritable rabbit's warren down there for her to hide in. That was assuming her invisibility spell did not hold, which it should. She should be doubly hidden from him.

She had been tired, but finding out the secret identity of a teacher who happened to share a classroom with her had set her entire body ablaze with adrenaline. There was no way she could sleep now. She had to stay and find out more about this Gentleman Lion.

Seventeen

September 21
Sunrise: 06:55
Sunset: 19:04
Moon: Waning Crescent
Daylight: 12:09 hours

DAHLIA RAN into the house and headed to the empty nooks in between books on one of the many massive bookshelves. Then she waited to see what the Gentleman Lion would do. She still held out hope for a stroke of luck. Perhaps the Lion would put down the Phoenix Egg that he had been carrying with him. She would recognize it if he put it on a table or in a case. But if he moved or touched anything, she would investigate it when he was gone just in case another object was somehow the Phoenix Egg in disguise.

The first thing Aaresh did was walk around the perimeter of his property, just inside the property line. She noted carefully where it was. His property not only included the round villa, but the bathhouse connected by a covered walkway and a garage. These were at the back of the property. After he finished investigating, and, to her satisfaction, gave no indication that he was able to find any trace of her scent (her invisibility spell should have concealed it) he went to a knob at the side of the house and turned it with his enormous forepaw.

Dahlia grew excited. Was this a secret lever to open a secret door? Was this the answer to how he had hidden the Phoenix Egg in plain sight?

No, apparently it was an outdoor faucet. He turned on the hose, stood up on his hind legs so he was bipedal, and watered his sunflowers. After that, he pulled a few weeds. He spoke words of encouragement to his plants in a deep, rumbling voice. He hummed a song to himself, almost like a purr, as he gardened.

It was so darn cute. Dahlia really wanted to pet him.

None of this was peculiar, as such, for a Shifter *in human form*. When Shifters were in human form, they behaved just like any other humans. They watered their plants, they sang songs, they talked to flowers that did not have brains and could not reply. The key phrase there was: *in human form*. Shifters did *not* do these things in their animal form.

But this Lion did.

Throughout the day, he moved from room to room in the strange and magnificent villa, doing things with the body of a lion that she would not have thought were physically possible, whether or not he had the intellectual capacity for it. All the rabbits in her family liked to embroider. Even the boy rabbit shifters had been taught the skill.

But they only did it as humans. Their little rabbity paws had no opposable thumb to hold a needle.

But the Lion fried himself an omelet from powdered eggs in his small bedroom kitchenette. He sat down at one of the tables in the courtyard and ate his breakfast primly with a knife and fork. Then he washed his paws in the outdoor sink. He did lick them clean, like a cat. But he also unbuttoned the cuffs of his dress shirt and rolled up his sleeves. He didn't take off the shirt; he just rolled up his sleeves.

Later, he went to the grand piano in the music room and began to play.

Music poured through the house like liquid gold. Dahlia felt her whole body quiver in response, like a sunflower turning toward the sun. He wasn't just *able* to play the piano. He was good. He was concert master level good. He played several classical pieces that she recognized although she could not name them. He also played some pop songs that she recognized, but he transformed them into something more complex and expressive than the original tune, making Shyla Ray's hit song, *"I wanna wanna wanna...all night long"* sound as though it could've been written by Mozart or Bach.

And then he began to play another song, not in the same way as he had played earlier pieces, but in fits and starts. Dahlia recognized the tune as the one he had been humming in the garden.

When she heard him mutter, "No, that's not right... Maybe it needs to go like this..." she realized that he wasn't simply *playing* a piece, he wasn't even *expanding* on a piece, he was *composing* a song from a seed.

He truly was a musical genius.

After he finished playing the piano, he picked up a cello.

He tucked the cello under his chin like a violin—the proportions worked—and played it that way. The sound was deep and organic and unique. The notes reverberated deep inside of her soul. She recognized that he was playing a melody that would be part of the song he was composing. Then, to her amazement, he moved from instrument to instrument about the room, playing different parts.

A human could've used a computer or a special electronic keyboard to compose and playback all the parts of a song together, but the Lion used magic. He returned to sit down at the piano, but he addressed the instruments in the room, commanding them: "Strings... Winds... Percussion... Begin!"

The instruments glowed with a halo of Elemental Fire and came to life, each automatically playing the part he had "taught" to each instrument. Like a conductor he raised a wand to lead the tempo. All of the instruments in the room repeated the section of the songs that he had played on them, and the full orchestra swirled with epic harmonies.

Dahlia didn't grow tired of watching him. He spent most of his afternoon in the Music Room, but it wasn't the only room he visited. He read books in the history collection. He spent a long time writing something in the Tragedy Room. He didn't like what he wrote. He crumbled it up and threw it in the trash. And then he went to the Comedy Room and started writing something there. He didn't use a computer or even a typewriter. He somehow gripped a large pen in his paw and wrote everything out by hand. By paw.

When it was safe, Dahlia crept to the trash can. She was still in rabbit form and of course still invisible. She had to switch back to human form, though she remained invisible, to pick the paper he'd crumbled out of the trash.

It was a screenplay. He had written a few scenes in just the time she had watched him. It was a dark piece about a child raised in a laboratory, tortured and lonely, but finding connection to the outside world through books and television and film and music. In the story, one of the few caretakers, a tutor that the child trusted, didn't show up one day and the little boy didn't know if his tutor had betrayed him or had been harmed because of their friendship. The scene ended abruptly.

It was absolutely heartbreaking. Why did he throw it away? It was a well written scene as far as she could judge things.

He threw away a Comedy scene too. She snuck into the trashcan and read that. It was the same story, but now the more tragic elements were disguised under a layer of black comedy. The underlying hurt was still there, but some of the jokes made her laugh out loud. She smothered her chuckles, although her spell made her inaudible as well as invisible.

He wrote something in the History Room too, although he didn't throw it away. Following him after he moved on to another part of the house, she flipped through the pages. It appeared to be an analysis of some incident during the Peloponnesian War. The level of detail was very academic and far beyond her meager knowledge of ancient Greek history.

Is there anything this Lion can't do? She wondered. Then she remembered the greasy omelet, and the fact that his kitchen appeared to have only two spices: salt and pepper. Obviously, he did not know how to cook.

But he did know how to fight. He went into the room

she thought of as the dojo, the one lined with weapons. He touched his forehead briefly to the handle of each weapon, and the weapon came alive, burning with a halo of golden light. Then he stepped into the center of the room on the mat and...

He ROARED.

The music had reverberated through her body in one way; the roar also affected her down to her bones, but the feeling of the mood his roar evoked was quite different. Every fiber of her being responded to the threat of a top predator. She froze in place and then bolted back into the bookcase where she cowered, quivering.

When she finally crept out, she found that he had not discovered her but was practicing in the gymnasium. Just as he had brought the musical instruments to life, he brought the swords and spears to life to fight him.

He controlled only one form of Elemental magic: Fire. Like her, he wielded only a single element. But like her, he had found unique and powerful ways to use that element. How many Fire Mages thought to use their power to record music on live instruments? How many Fire Mages animated weapons to fly through the air and attack on their own? These were extremely specialized applications of a broad category. She knew from experience how long it took to cultivate such specialization.

The day was passing and the one thing he had not done in all this time was give any indication of where the Phoenix Egg was hidden.

Someone was in his house. Someone was hunting him.

Aaresh wasn't certain at first. He started with a little

uneasiness at the back of his mind, nervousness that raised the hackles on the back of his neck. Long experience with paranoia proving to be just extreme prudence meant that he did not dismiss the feeling even when he had nothing else to go on for a long time. He also gave no indication of his nervousness, so as not to tip off the hunter that he was aware of his presence, if indeed there was a hunter.

He found an excuse to go into every room in his house. He even worked on his screenplay, which was loosely based on his own life, though he couldn't concentrate, and everything he wrote was utter crap. He did get a funny scene out of it when he tried to rewrite it as a comedy. That just showed that, in the grand scheme of things, he would better serve humanity as someone to point at and laugh at rather than a person anyone could relate to. He wanted to have the Lion character wearing clothing, because he knew that would make it even funnier, but it wasn't historically accurate. He didn't start wearing clothing in his lion form until he lived on his own.

Thinking about historical accuracy inspired him to add some more pages to his magnum opus about the Peloponnesian War. His premise was that the Greek city states had destroyed themselves through lack of ability to trust one another. If Sparta and Athens had not each betrayed the trust of the other, Greek civilization would not have fallen from a Golden Age into a Dark Age. He had sought publication through the academic process and was told by his peer review feedback that his thesis was not original.

That infuriated him. The actual writing and research was *completely* original, and, in fact, included sources that humans had not seen for over two thousand five hundred years because the pertinent scrolls had been kept in other Spheres. The fact that other scholars, using less extensive sources, had independently concluded the same thing as he had did not invalidate his thesis! Did the foolish human scholars want to know the truth or did they only care about being "original," regardless of whether the "original" claims were valid or blithering nonsense?!

For a long time after he had received those rejection letters he stopped working on the book, but today he felt inspired again.

Not inspired really. He just needed to keep himself busy while he tried to find the intruder.

In the Philosophy Room, he found another abandoned project, his thesis that Nietzsche had secretly been a Lion Shifter whose parents had forbidden him to take his alter form, until finally, the inability to shift had driven the Shifter mad. The paper was a Philosophy essay rather than a History essay, because, alas, Aaresh had no solid proof that Nietzche was a Shifter, only speculation. Therefore, he analyzed Nietzsche's concept of "the blond beast," as a crypto-confession of a Lion Shifter.

"'At the center of all these noble races *the Beast of prey*,' Nietzsche had written before his mental breakdown, 'the splendid *Blond Beast* avidly *prowling around* for spoil and victory; this *hidden center* needs release from time to time, the *Beast must out again*, must *return to the wild*—Roman, Arabian, Germanic, Japanese nobility, Homeric heroes, Scandinavian Vikings—in this requirement they are all alike.' To which Aaresh Raj addended, "Like other Romantics, Nietzsche overreacted to the strictures of the Enlightenment, rejecting the 'shackles' of civilization in order to free the suppressed animal side of his Shifter nature.... But in rejecting the human half of himself, he lost his mind, his reason, his moral anchor, his conscience, and unleashed the unbridled rage of the unchecked, inflamed, hunted, hunting, rabid animal. Much as those later movements that claimed him as a prophet unleashed a period in human history of unbridled, diseased violence that washed a continent in blood and murder…"

Aaresh stared at what he had written, laboriously, with a pen in his paw. He had never finished this essay because the conclusion, that the proper philosophy required a balance of beast and man, of culture and instinct, pained him too much. He himself had no such balance.

He went to the Poetry Room and sat down to write a sonnet about why people wore clothes. A human didn't *need* clothes any more than a lion did, he wrote—in iambic pentameter—it was the sense of shame, the knowledge that you were so much less than the people around you, that made you want to add something to yourself, that made you want to hide and mask yourself. Clothing allowed shapeshifting without magic. Clothing allowed the ugly duckling to be reborn like a phoenix, to burn away one old identity and embrace a new one. That was why he wore clothes even as a lion.

He tried to capture all of that in a poem. Just like the screenplay, his words were utter trash, and he threw the draft away.

The hunter was using an invisibility spell. Or, more properly speaking, an *insensibility spell*: it affected all senses. In that manner, it was like his glamour, which acted on every physical sense in the earthly Sphere to disguise him. But while his glamour was like a theatrical costume, merely changing his role in the grand narrative, whoever he was seeking was off-stage completely.

That was the only explanation for why Aaresh had not been able to see or hear or smell the intruder.

And yet he was *certain* the hunter was there.

The hunter is too smart to be a Shifter, he thought. No Shifter could hide their smell that well from me. It must be one of the Azir themselves, or else a Witch or Mage of adept level magic.

But Aaresh had spent a lifetime being spied on, being tricked, probed, tested, deceived, and manipulated. He had developed a loathing for every evil form of deception. The only lies he loved were those of a child's imagination writ large: the lies of the theater, the cinema, of novels and video games. Those were lies, but they did not trick you out of any truth you owned. The lies of the Arts only enticed you to forget the desolation of reality long enough to endure another day. At its best, every great story was not a lie at all, but a great truth wrapped in a metaphor. A great story was a path to liberation from suffering because it led you to that great truth by tiny, tiny steps.

The lies of a hunter were not to liberate you, but to enslave you. Aaresh knew hunters. He was exquisitely sensitive to all of their tricks. Within his breast, avidly prowling around for spoil and victory, the darkness at his hidden center waited for him to release it.

I'm going to find you, you bastard, he promised silently. You will learn what it means to be prey. You will cringe in fear. You will run from the unleashed beast.

Something changed.

Dahlia didn't know what it was, but suddenly every hair on her rabbit body stood on end. *Leave!* screamed her rabbit instinct. *Leave now!*

The Gentleman Lion was not as tame as he pretended.

For once, she didn't argue with her inner animal's fear.

Dahlia waited until Aaresh turned his back and she dashed away. Just as she did, he turned around and erupted into a terrible roar. Unlike his roar in the dojo, which had just been practice, this bellow thundered with rage.

Somehow, he had detected her, and he was furious.

She was still invisible, and she was still in rabbit form. He leapt, trying to pounce on someone he couldn't see, which meant he had guessed that she was using an invisibility spell. But from the place he landed, she could tell he still expected a much larger opponent, someone at least as tall as a human or Elf.

The Empress was right. No one ever expected to be hunted by a cute, fluffy bunny.

Dahlia escaped the villa.

She ran all the way home and then she collapsed in her bed. But all night she was tormented by nightmares in which she did not escape but was caught between his paws. She kept asking him, *How did you know I was there? How did you know?*

Eighteen

September 22, Autumn Equinox
Sunrise: 06:56
Sunset: 19:03
Moon: Waning Crescent
Daylight: 12:07

DAHLIA HADN'T SUCCEEDED in finding the Doomsday Weapon. However, she had found out an incredible amount of information about her target. She now knew that he was hiding in plain sight, as a school teacher at a private academy for elementary through high school aged students. Many arcanes in Arcana Glen sent their children to the school. What would they think if they knew the nerdy and academic centaur teaching English literature was a mutant Sun Lion raised by mad scientists, who had stolen a Doomsday device that could destroy the Earth?

Were the children in any danger from him? She didn't

want to think so. But she couldn't leave the question unanswered. Also, she needed to see him during the school day to see if he had, perhaps, however unlikely it seemed, stored the Phoenix Egg in his classroom.

Of course, if he had, then the compass should have led her to the school grounds rather than to his villa. She couldn't understand why the target moved around. He must change its hiding place frequently. If that were true, then even if he wasn't actually carrying it in his pocket, she still had to trail him to see if she could catch him when he moved it.

She thought about going to the school as herself. She could test if he knew she was the one hunting him. But she would have to give some excuse for seeing him, aside from the reason closest to the truth, that before she discovered he was her target in a Bounty Hunt, she had been interested in him as a man. Admitting that now was out of the question. She couldn't date someone she had to hunt; it was a conflict of interest.

Not to mention, just a really, really bad idea.

The easiest and most obvious solution was to maintain her invisibility cloak of mist and fog. But that had risks too. Somehow, he had detected her despite her invisibility.

How?

She had no idea, but she did know one thing. The more opportunity she gave for him to study her magic, the more likely he was to find a way to counter it. Since she didn't know what he was doing to counter her spell to begin with, she couldn't counter his counter.

She didn't have any other form of invisibility spell to use, though, so she decided she would have to risk it.

It was strange walking on the campus during the day. She had gone to the public High School herself. She'd never attended a fancy private school like this. What would it have been like? At her school, she had to hide the fact she was a rabbit shifter, because most of the other students and teachers were human. She had her sister and several cousins and some friends that knew about magic, so she wasn't completely alone, but it still wasn't the same as going to a school where magic was openly taught.

She was used to avoiding people when she was invisible. It took a special skill set, because although most people weren't aware of it, normally when two people walked toward each other, both took some effort to avoid a collision. When you were invisible, you couldn't count on the other person doing anything to avoid walking smack into you. Although her Water magic did affect touch, it had its limits. If somebody bumped into her, they would know something was there. They would be able to wipe away her misty magic cloak, and feel her body, even if they still couldn't see it. She had to avoid that disaster.

When she was inside the classroom, she turned into her bunny form, still invisible, and hopped up on to a file cabinet in the far corner. This was unlikely to be in anyone's way. In fact, based on the thin layer of dust, it was unlikely to be in the way of even a janitor's washcloth.

Throughout the day, she stayed there and watched Mr Raj the Centaur teach class after class, to students ranging in age from Fifth Graders to High School seniors.

He was a wonderful teacher. He was funny and kind to the younger kids, stern but inspiring with the older kids. He had a self-deprecating humor, a little dark, similar to what she had seen in the comedy screenplay that he had thrown in the trash. But he also brought subjects alive. The way he talked about characters and stories or events in ancient history made it seem as though they were his best friends.

Now that she knew what to look for, Dahlia noted how Aaresh gave away little hints about his past all the time.

He told the kids at one point, "Even if you were raised in a basement by sociopaths, with books you will always have a family worthy of love. You may think that they can't love you back, but they can. Love means giving completely of yourself without holding back, giving the gift of truth. And books do that for us. They give their gift completely; they don't care who you are, or what your body looks like, or what your background is, your sex or your race or your kingdom.

"Books show you that you aren't the only one who has doubts, feelings of inadequacy, or challenges, quests, and tragedies. Some people will try to tell you that because you are a Shifter, you can't understand a book written by a Witch, or if you are a human magic user or even a human with no magic at all, that you can't understand the point of view of an Elf or a Nymph...That's nonsense.

"I am a Centaur, not an ordinary human man. I'm not an ancient Greek warrior. I don't need to be any of those to understand Achilles or Hector or Odysseus. You don't have to belong to a specific tribe in order to read a book; by reading a book, you create and join a new tribe, the tribe of everyone else who has read that book. From that point forward, no matter what else divides you, that book ties you to them. You have at least one slender bridge between you and other people. And you can forge a friendship across that bridge if you choose to cross it.

"There's no magic as powerful as words..." Here he paused and cocked his head and added, "Except for music. Story is music without sound, and music is a story made of sound."

Dahlia didn't know about the students, but this impassioned speech made her think of the hard-bound gold-embossed editions of the Iliad and Odyssey that she had on the shelf at home, more as a decoration, like the glass swan that sat next to them, than as actual books she ever intended to read. Maybe she would crack one of those volumes open after she finished this case. Or maybe she would catch the movie version about the battle of Troy with that really hot actor... Yeah, that might be more her style.

She didn't think she moved or did anything to drop her invisibility spell, but just at that moment he looked directly at the corner of the room on top of the file cabinet where she was sitting.

Aaresh was pontificating about his love of books, probably going on for much too long, and boring his students, when suddenly he had that same impression as he had experienced in his house yesterday. The sense that someone was watching him, hunting him. He jerked his head toward the corner of the room where he half expected to see the hidden glint of a lens, a video camera watching and recording him.

But that was just a habit left over from the life he left behind. Wasn't it?

Just to be certain, he decided that as soon as the students were gone, after the last bell, he would once again check the entire classroom for wires and cameras. He had done so before he moved in, but it didn't hurt to keep vigilant.

Fortunately, he had a special ability, which he had developed all on his own, ensuring that even his former captors did not know about it, which enabled him to detect such surveillance devices.

However, when the last bell rang, an adult man entered the classroom. He was a stranger, someone whom Aaresh had never met. A Shifter, but of course at this school, that was almost a given. The man's Animal was either a Dog or a Wolf. He wore some kind of musk that muted his scent. Again, when Shifters were among many different kinds of arcanes, that was something the predators, especially, tried to do, to reduce the fear they instilled in those who had prey animals as their alters.

"I'm looking for Lindsay," the man said. "My niece?"

Lindsay was one of Aarush's students from fourth period. Another teacher might have spontaneously shared that information, but Aaresh was too cautious. Just because someone was looking for Lindsay didn't mean that someone was someone with the right to find her. In order to make certain this was a parental guardian looking for her and not a predator, Aaresh said, "It's best to check directly with the office. They can help you."

"Thank you, sir." The man smiled, not seeming offended by the answer.

Dahlia hopped down from the file cabinet and dashed out the door. She had seen the exchange between Aeresh and the strange man. She followed the stranger when he left the classroom, her sensitive nose quivering, trying to identify his animal through the heavy cologne he used to disguise it.

Hellhound. Dammit, he was probably another bounty hunter. What were the chances that a Hellhound just *happened* to be interested in the same man she was tracking?

In case he was actually innocent and really only looking

for his niece Lindsay, Dahlia followed him to see if he went to the office as Aaresh had suggested.

Nope. The Hellhound went to the parking lot toward a sleek black car.

He was about to get in when he was confronted by another man who had been deliberately hiding behind the car.

Dahlia knew this second man; it was Zachary Gnaw-fang, a student from her class. What was Zachary's connection to the Hellhound? Were they working together?

Evidently not. The tension between the two men was as electric as a live wire around a penitentiary. Still invisible, Dahlia watched the confrontation.

"I know who you are and what you did," snarled Zachary. "Since I also know who you work for, I'm going to give you one morning before I rip out your throat. Stay away."

"I don't answer to you, *dog*," sneered the Hellhound. "I'm my own master. But that's something you wouldn't really understand, is it?"

The Hellhound walked right up to Zachary and grabbed his long-sleeved shirt, ripping the right sleeve in one swift motion to reveal a silver brand on Zachary's right bicep.

Quietly and inaudibly, Dahlia gasped. The silver brand was a sign that Zachary was owned, like a dog, or a pet, as the Hellhound had implied. It meant he belonged to the Winter Elves.

She had known that Zachary was a Wolf Shifter. But she had never seen his wolf, and there was no way to tell the color of his fur from his smell. The brand hain made it perfectly clear. Zachary was a White Wolf. It was highly likely that he was one of the pack who had chased her in the forest because they thought she had killed one of them.

Zachary snarled. His whole body shimmered with magic, as if he were about to shift, and his mouth briefly elongated into a snout with long teeth, but he resisted a full transformation.

"You're on the leash of demons," Zachary snapped. "You're worse than me."

"My masters are superior to yours," said the Hellhound, "As I am superior to you. Your masters had their chance to catch the mark, and you failed. Now it's my turn. I won't fail. And I won't let you get in my way."

"You're the one who killed my pack brother!" shouted Zachary.

"Consider it a warning not to get between me and my mark again," sneered the Hellhound. "The prize is *mine*."

He shoved Zachary, who once again, almost shifted, but the Hellhound walked away, smirking, as if confident the White Wolf wouldn't follow. And he was right. The Hellhound disappeared into the forest, but Zachary made no move to follow. Zachary made a sound close to a howl of frustration but he slammed open the door to his car, slammed the door shut again, and tore out of the parking lot with a screeching of burning tires.

And it also seemed highly likely that they were after the same thing she was. Aaresh and the Phoenix Egg.

The Hellhound, the White Wolves and her; they were all after the Sun Lion and the Doomsday Weapon he was hiding.

Nineteen

September 22, Autumn Equinox
Sunrise: 06:56
Sunset: 19:03
Moon: Waning Crescent
Daylight: 12:07

NOW THAT DAHLIA knew she had competition, she had to work faster. It was time to up the ante.

She didn't waste any more time trying to follow Aaresh today. She needed to trap him, and she wasn't going to do it by arm wrestling. She needed to use the tools the Empress and Emperor had given her.

She raced back to the secret villa in the woods. Careful to keep outside the perimeter that would probably trigger his defensive spells, she poured Elemental Water from the magic flask in a circle around the house. She made certain that the end point met up with the beginning so that the circle was complete. She knew the circle was finished when the water lifted into the air and glowed radiant aquamarine.

She could feel the Elemental Water responding to her will, ready when she needed it to snap shut like a clam, forming a perfect spherical cage around the house. Now she set the trap so that the cage would automatically shut even if something happened to her.

She didn't want to imprison Aaresh, but at this point she was running out of options. Fortunately, it was only noon. She had one last chance to check his villa for the Phoenix Egg before he came home from school at 3 o'clock.

Aaresh decided to return home early from school. It was the Autumn Equinox. Technically, there were still a few more minutes of sunlight than darkness in the day, because sunrise was measured from when the tip-top of the sun first peaked over the Eastern horizon to when the last of the sun dipped below the Western horizon.

But Aaresh felt the shift in his power, as the dark half of the year asserted itself.

Whoever had been at his house had also tracked him to his school. But whatever magic they used to conceal themselves was stronger than his ability to penetrate it.

Or was it? If there were multiple operatives, that meant there could be somebody at his home even now, searching it while he was gone.

He thought he had a way to uncover whatever they were using to conceal themselves, but he didn't want to do it in public. If he could just capture one member of the team, he would force that individual to deliver up the rest.

No matter what it took, he would never go back to captivity.

~

Dahlia searched the villa quickly but once again she saw no sign of the Phoenix Egg.

Then one of her magical alarms warned her that Aaresh was already on his way back home.

Dang it! She thought she would have more time. She had to get out of here. He had already pulled his big car up into the drive and entered the perimeter of the house. She had to escape before her trap sprang. Not that she would be ensnared by her own shield. She was the only one immune to it and would be able to walk in and out of it anytime she wanted. For *him*, it would be like a solid iron wall; for *her* it would be like a heavy fog. It might look solid, but she would walk right through it.

But as soon as the trap closed on him, he would know she was there.

And he would be *furious*.

She raced to the perimeter of the house.

A wall of flames rows in front of her so quickly that her bunny fur was singed. She flailed backwards. Too late!

He had also built a trap! His trap was made with Elemental Fire instead of Elemental Water. The heat from the shimmering golden shield, which she could see only when she was in proximity to it, was so intense that she had to drag herself away.

At a yard from the wall, it was invisible to her, but the burn she had suffered from touching it remained.

She dragged herself back inside the house to lick her

wounds and try to heal. Now she hoped he would not get stuck in her trap because then the two of them...

The two of them would *both* be trapped. Inside. Together.

She heard the soft footfalls of the giant Lion.

As he was nearing his house, Aaresh saw the trap he had set burst into flame and create a sphere of intense heat and light all around his house. Of course, only the top portion of the hollow sphere was visible because the other half would be under the earth. There was no way anyone was going to escape that ball of fire.

He was smugly congratulating himself as he passed harmlessly through the fire. To him it was only like smoke, or opaque and dark, but easy to pass through.

He only realized his mistake when something snapped behind him and he felt shards of ice needle his flesh, so cold that it burned. He yelled and leapt forward to escape the wall of ice that rose all around him.

He knew exactly what had happened because the spell was the mirror of his own, only made out of water instead of fire. He was trapped inside his own house, with the same hunter who had set a trap for him.

The two of them were now trapped in the same prison together.

His golden eyes narrowed down to slits of rage. Aaresh had been locked in cells with those who wished him harm before. When he was forced to kill to entertain his guards or to get rid of someone they didn't like as a favor to them, he had always resisted murdering his cell mate, and yet he had always been driven to it by the fact the other prisoner would attack him first, out of fear.

This time, no one was urging him to kill, but he didn't need to be urged. He hated the hunter who had come for him.

Two entered this arena, but only one would emerge.

~

"Welcome to my home, Hunter," the deep voice of the lion said sarcastically. "I know why you are here."

Dahlia was still in pain and hiding in the darkest, smallest, space she could find between two books in one of the shelves around the outer edge of his home library. His deep voice was so loud that when he projected his voice she could hear him anywhere in the house. He wasn't in the room with her, but he didn't need to be for her to hear every word he enunciated clearly.

He was enraged but calm.

He claimed to know what she had come for. Did he know she wanted the Phoenix Egg? Was there any chance they could just discuss this like two civilized adults? If she explained the danger, might he simply hand the Doomsday device to her?

"You will not get what you want," he assured her loudly. "Nor will you leave this place alive."

Well, dang.

The situation was not looking good. With that kind of attitude, she had to assume he was working with the bad guys. Her best bet was to stay hidden and stay invisible.

He first walked the circuit of the nine rooms on the lower floor. When his walk around did not reveal anything to him, she sighed with relief.

But then he began to shine.

There was really no other word for it. She had seen Seraphs glowing before. They really were surrounded by a halo of light, not just around their heads, but around their entire bodies. She had seen Pixies sparkle. And when Elemental magic was performed, it usually created bright, colorful sparks when the spell was at its peak.

But the luminosity coming from the Sun Lion outshone all of them. He radiated a great golden light, more brilliant than the gentle nimbus around a Seraph, more dazzling than the sparkle of pixie dust, with greater clarity than the light from any spell she'd ever seen.

But even more alarming was that the light from his corona revealed things that had formerly been invisible. Works of art that she had not noticed while hopping around the room were now suddenly apparent. Extra stair-cases and even hidden doors that had been concealed by magic became outlined and obvious in the light from his corona. The shimmering light flowing from his body was not just a big flashlight. It was a kind of truth spell, a light to reveal hidden things.

Hidden things... Like her. The Fire magic in his corona was extremely powerful, and she was not confident the refractive camouflage of her Water magic would stand up to it. More likely her invisibility would evaporate like morning dew under a rising sun.

Systematically, he moved around each of the rooms, illuminating the shadowed places and hidden spots with the light from his body. Then he systematically began to move the bookcases, rolling each one out of the way to create an aisle between them so he could illuminate all the dark nooks and hidden crevices.

"I realize," he said, conversationally, but with an aura of

menace underneath his words, "That you are not only invisible but must have a size altering spell as well. Perhaps you are a Leprechaun or a Pixie and can make yourself as small as a child's doll. It doesn't matter. I know every inch of this house. It is my home. It is my den. You cannot hide from me here."

He was getting closer and closer to the bookshelf where she was crouching. Her burns still stung, although her body was fighting as hard as it could to heal. As he moved each shelf along the track, the metal shelves groaned and screeched, a sound that made her shudder. Waiting for him to finally open the bookshelf and show light upon her hiding space was terrifying.

Finally, she started to hop.

There were enough spaces between the books on the half empty shelves that she was able to move from shelf to shelf ahead of him. But he was close enough to her now that his radiance touched her body through the shelves. She had hoped that if the light itself could not penetrate the heavy iron bookshelves that she would be safe, but obviously the emanations that came from him were not just visual. They radiated in all spectrums across all the senses and through magic as well.

The Lion smiled.

When a lion smiles, it is a baring of fangs. Not a pleasant sight.

"I have shined upon your spell and broken it, Hunter. I can hear and smell you now. So... You are a... rabbit."

She kept hopping, trying to stay ahead of him, but he surprised her by loping ahead, anticipating the shelf she would run to next.

It suddenly opened before her, and he stood there in

the aisle between the shelves. She made the mistake of looking directly into the light and it almost blinded her.

She leapt, trying to escape further into the darkness, but a paw smacked her out of the air, and she hit the ground. Another paw came down on the other side of her. One of his huge, curved claws pinned her fur.

His laughter created a hurricane in her face, blowing her ears and her back. "I have you now, little bunny."

She switched to human form, bringing her clothes with her from the ether. Now instead of her fur, her cargo pants were pinned to the ground.

The Lion blinked at her in shock. "Dahlia Moon? *You* are the one hunting me?"

She had never expected to see a look of such hurt and betrayal on the face of a lion.

Twenty

September 22, Autumn Equinox
Sunrise: 06:56
Sunset: 19:03
Moon: Waning Crescent
Daylight: 12:07

BY THIS POINT in his life, he should've been used to betrayal, Aaresh thought bitterly.

His shock was his enemy's opportunity. Dahlia grabbed a knife and cut a hole in cargo pants around his claw and leaped, switching back to bunny form in the air and literally running over the fur of his back and across the room.

Awareness that the whole time the pretty little schoolteacher had been hunting him cut him like a knife. Nothing was an accident, now he was certain of that. The fact that she shared a classroom with him. The fact that she had supposedly run into him at the festival. The fact that she asked him to fight with her.

He reeled inside. He had fought side-by-side with this woman! The whole time she was probably studying him to learn his weaknesses. The contest had never mattered to her. It had all been about him from the start; there was no other explanation.

"How long have you been hunting me?" Aaresh demanded. He sniffed the air trying to follow her trail. But as soon as she had escaped the circumference of his radiance, her insensibility spell had kicked back in. He could no longer hear her movements or smell which direction she had gone. He would have to start all over again, systematically, as he had before.

"No matter how many times you run from me, I will eventually wear you down," Aaresh warned her. "I bet you need sleep. Maybe you don't need it right now, but eventually you will. I don't know whether rabbits are diurnal or nocturnal, but one way or another you'll tire and shut your eyes and rest your body. But me? Here's something I bet your masters didn't tell you...

"I don't need sleep," he smirked. "It was just one of the many experiments they did to see if they could make me into some kind of super-soldier-monster. Not only am I more powerful than an ordinary Shifter, and more intelligent, and more educated, but I don't sleep. Ever."

He padded forward, shining brightly, searching carefully.

"Maybe you're thinking that the light I am emitting, the radiation that destroys your insensibility spell will eventually flicker out and become an ember and finally die from exhaustion. That would happen with any other ordinary Fire spell. But it won't happen to me. I can shine all day long. My light is to an ordinary Fire spell what the nuclear fires of the sun are a campfire. It's a form of energy unlike anything any other Shifter can access. I bet your masters didn't warn you about that either."

"I don't wish to fight you, Aaresh," her voice called out.

Aaresh heard her reply, but with her insensibility spell cloaking her again, he couldn't pinpoint the direction it came from. He had to hand it to her, her concealment illusion was a work of art. Not as good as his Corona of Clarity, but extremely good, nonetheless.

"If you don't wish to fight me, then don't try to trap me. Undo the shield you built around my home. I'll undo my shield and let you go."

"Give me the Phoenix Egg and you have a deal!" she called back.

He furrowed his brow. He had her talking now, but he wasn't going to let that distract him from his search. He kept padding softly through the rooms. He had realized that he did not need to illuminate every corner to find her. All he had to do was get close enough to her that he could counter her spell. By smell alone, he would be able to find her.

"I don't know what you're talking about," he said. "I don't have any Phoenix Egg. I would never steal the young of another sentient creature."

"I know you have it," she said. "I have a way to track it and I tracked it to you. Multiple times."

"I don't have it."

"You're lying. Just like you're lying about letting me go if I take down my spell. You are planning to kill me. Maybe you can't smell me, but I can smell you. I smell your rage and I can sense your predation. I can smell you hunting me."

"I just want to talk," he lied. He continued to hunt her, just as she accused.

"Put the egg down where I can grab it and then back away. Drop your spell first and then I will drop mine."

"So you can betray me again?"

"Betray you *again*? I never betrayed you!"

"Your entire approach to me was under false pretenses. You befriended me only to capture me."

"No! I only want you to give something back that you stole!"

"You mean to steal from me."

"I won't have to steal it if you just give it to me!"

He had to laugh at that. There was an edge of bitterness in his laughter, however. She was a brazen little bunny thief, wasn't she?

"Just give me the Phoenix Egg, Aaresh."

"Your masters are lying to you, bunny. There is no Phoenix Egg. It was always *me* they wanted. Maybe they had to trick you into hunting me. If you are truly a dupe in this, I will let you go. You can still walk away."

Even as he said it, however, he wondered if he dared let her go. She already knew too much about him...

Somehow, she knew what he was thinking. Or maybe it was obvious to her that he planned to betray her, because she was also planning to betray him.

"You intend to hunt me down and kill me," said Dahlia from her hiding spot. "I can sense your murderous rage. You already told me several of your secret powers that your masters don't know about, and you think I expect you will let me go? I know you won't!"

"Then we are at an impasse," he said. "And there is no more point talking about it."

After that he grew silent. Aaresh focused his concentration inside. He focused on the corona of radiance he called his "Shine." He had never needed it much, beyond examining his art collection for hidden dimensions. He had used it to find a few secret passageways and extra stairways in his house. In fact, originally his home had been hidden from public view and he had used his Shine to find it in the first place, and then to contact the original owner and make a bid on it. She had been quite surprised that he had been aware of its existence.

But now he wondered: how far could he push his corona? It was a relatively new power to him, something he had only discovered after he escaped captivity. He had never experimented with it as he had with all his other abilities. Perhaps it was time to start.

He sat down and closed his eyes and focused on shining brighter and brighter and brighter. Soon the rays of his corona reached every wall of the house and then all the way to the perimeter and then all the way to the shields—his and hers—that surrounded the property.

He heard her spell shatter like glass on the floor. Then he had her scent and he raced toward it.

Dahlia ran, but it was too late. Once again, the Lion pounced on her and captured her between his paws. By now the light coming from him was so bright that she could not even look at him. She squirmed and bucked, but she could not escape. She was so tiny in this form compared to him that he could bite her head off. He could swallow her whole.

"Shift!" Aaresh commanded. "Shift back into human, Dahlia! I'm not going to kill you as an animal!"

She shifted. "What difference does it make? You're going to kill me either way!"

His fangs were as long as her entire head—and that was when she was in human form. It would've been trivial for him to bite her. He could've also pierced her heart with one of his claws. Heck, he could probably *shake* her to death.

But he stared at her with his huge gold eyes. She could still smell anger on him, but her sense of empathy no longer detected the predator mindset. Something much more complex and convoluted was going on inside his mind.

"I'm not a killer," he said, almost regretfully. "I am not the one who does that. That's *his* job. You'll have to wait until *he* comes. Then I am afraid that nothing can save you."

She was still trapped between his enormous paws. "What are you talking about?"

"You and I are not the only ones trapped inside this villa. There is another. You see a Lion, a top predator. But I am not the true Top Predator in the wild. There is another animal even more dangerous than I. The scientists who experimented on me destroyed my natural ability to shapeshift and changed it into something even more deadly and dangerous. This form you see... *This* is my harmless form. My *civilized* form. I change into something worse at night."

"Do you mean.... a Dragon?" It was the only predator she could think of that topped a Lion.

The Lion laughed. The deep rumbling sound was almost like a purr, and it tickled her.

"No," he said in his deep strange voice. "Not a Dragon. You still aren't thinking dangerous enough. Consider the worst beast on this planet. The most savage, the most lethal, the most relentless."

"A vampire? A demon?"

"You're so naïve."

She wasn't certain how he smirked at her with a lion's muzzle, but the expression was as clear as his rage before. He had an incredibly expressive face.

"You'll see soon enough." He opened his paws.

Was he actually letting her go? Or was this a cat and mouse game? Did he want her to run just so he could pounce on her third time?

"I have no need to hold you," Aaresh declared. "When he arrives, he will find you even more easily than I have. I have too many conflicts of conscience to kill someone in cold blood, especially a young woman such as yourself. No matter what you've done to me, I can't bring myself to hurt you. But the beast will not share my hesitation. He has none. He has killed many, many people, bunny."

"You talk about him like he's another person, but you just admitted it's another form of you."

"You must know that some Shifters have no control over their bestial side."

"Yes, I understand that, but a Shifter is expected to gain control of his animal by the time he's an adult!"

"The only way I can control him is to lock him up. But he's slippery. Even better at escape than you are. You can save yourself if you lower the cage you built around my house. Otherwise... I will let him run free." The Lion bared his fangs. "I am not locked in here with you. You are locked in here with him."

Twenty-One

September 22, Autumn Equinox
Sunrise: 06:56
Sunset: 19:03
Moon: Waning Crescent
Daylight: 12:07 hours

DAHLIA WANTED TO HIDE, but what good would it do?

Aaresh roamed the house restlessly. He ignored Dahlia. After a while, he sat down at the grand piano and began to play.

What was the point of hiding from him any longer? He could break her spell anytime he wanted. Usually her small size enabled her to escape a predator like him but his feline body was so limber that he was able to fit into spaces his bulk shouldn't have allowed.

Dahlia pushed her magic against the limits of the shields enclosing the villa, or rather, *his* Fire shield. How much did the Fire Shield limit her action *inside* the villa? Could she still create a Water Rope to do her Climb to the Moon trick? Maybe. She could still access the leylines of Elemental Water, although it felt like the power poured through a tiny funnel. She *could* still access her compass. And she could even still access her weapon, the crossbow. She wasn't powerless. But she wasn't prepared yet to fight Aaresh until she had some assurance she could win.

She remembered bitterly how easily the Centaur had been tossed against the side of the stadium during the fight, leaving the last forty minutes of the battle entirely to her. If he had assumed his true form, and used his limberness, along with his other natural weapons and Sun magic, instead of pretending to be a Demi-shifter, a prey animal, he could have finished the fight with her. Perhaps if he had combined her skills with his own, they would have even come close to *defeating* the Empress and Emperor.

In fact, she was starting to wonder exactly how powerful Aaresh was. His captors wanted to make him into a Super-Soldier-Monster. What if they had succeeded? If he had used the radiant power of his body to make blinding light... He could have taken on the whole arena by himself, blinding any arcane who tried to fight him.

He had even mentioned that the power was *nuclear*, not like any normal earthly combustion. Dragons were immune to fire, but you could kill one with a nuke. If that was true, then Aaresh was possibly the strongest Shifter she had ever met.

The true King of the Beast Shifters.

And yet he claimed that the form he would soon turn into at nightfall was worse....

There were many questions she wanted to ask Aaresh, but he was now determined to ignore her.

She went into the music room, where he was playing the piano. She sat against one wall, facing him with her knees drawn up under her chin. She listened to him play.

He glanced at her only once and then carefully avoided looking at her again.

She closed her eyes and let the music wash over her. She should be checking his shield for weaknesses or preparing her weapons for a trick, but the music soothed and entranced her. While he was playing, it was easy to forget anything horrible in the past or any worries about the future. All that mattered was now, the beauty of this moment, the infinity of sadness and tenderness in the song.

The music he chose to play was a mix of classical and contemporary songs that she recognized as soundtracks of movies. But every piece had in common that it was unbearably sad. She wasn't educated enough in music to recognize all the pieces, but she did recognize the music of Leos Janacek, because it had been used in the soundtrack of a movie she liked, *The Unbearable Lightness of Being*.

"You know," she said conversationally, "I read that book and I never understood it. I never even understood the phrase in the title. But now, having met you, I can't think of a better phrase. You, your existence in this place, it makes me think of the unbearable lightness of being. Or am I taking it too literally?"

He smashed his paws on the piano making a discordant sound. He glared at her with his enormous lambent eyes. "You should be staying as far away from me as possible."

"Why? You said I'm in no danger from you, only from the other one."

The Lion glared at her. "Most people make the mistake of being more frightened of me in this form."

"You're wearing a silk vest, trousers and playing the

piano. I'm sorry if I'm not afraid of you in this form, but you make it difficult."

He snarled. It was a very bestial sound.

He glanced down at his piano. "You are right."

"About what?"

"You completely failed to understand the book, *The Unbearable Lightness of Being*. Lightness in the book's context has nothing to do with illumination, it has to do with gravity. The theory of gravity refers to the philosophy of the ancient Greek Parmenides, who claimed that gravity is a negative. Philosophically, gravity also refers to the Nietzschean idea that time is cyclical. The ancients looked at the cycles of the moon and the sun, and assumed that there would be an eternal return of every moment that exists, in the same way that Spring returns every year, the Full Moon returns every month, and the Sun returns every day.

"In contrast, Parmenides argued that the cyclical nature of the seasons is an illusion, because the Eternal Return is really a spiral, progressing inevitably toward the heat death of the universe. Every new year, month, and day is not really a return but an entirely new set of moments which are fragile and fleeting, unique and temporary. Therefore, the only thing we can do in life is to live in the beauty of the Eternally Unique, appreciating each moment as it blooms and dies and will never exist again."

"Ah," said Dahlia. "Is *that* what that movie was about? In that case, I guess you're right. I did *not* get that at all. I thought it was about the fact that all men, whether mundane or arcane, behave like Tom Rabbits, using any bullshit excuse to cheat on their mates."

A snort very much like a laugh came from the Lion.

But then he glanced at the ticking clock, and the sun beams, which streamed into every room in the house through large skylights. The spotlight created by the sunroof had been moving across the floor all late afternoon and now it had reached the edge of the room and started to redden with the deepness of sunset.

"The sun sets at three minutes past seven today," he said. "Then the darkness brings the beast. You should live another day, Bunny. Take down your shield. Promise to leave me alone. And I will let you go. Let me let you live."

She was tempted to cut and run. Would the Emperor and Empress really blame her if she went back to them and explained that she was outmatched by a giant, nuclear-powered Lion Shifter? Who could blame her for that?

If she had been here only to prove her own worth, she probably would have run. She could swallow her pride and admit when she was weak. No matter what he said about opportunities not returning, in her experience, there was always tomorrow to try again, next month or next year. Opportunity did come in cycles.

But the talk about the fleetingness and fragility of life also reminded her that some things could never be undone. When a nuclear bomb triggered fusion, it created the heat of a thousand suns. It was an interesting metaphor for their current situation, trapped together in a tight space, forced to get closer to an enemy who could destroy her with light. She would have liked to ask what he thought about the unbearable lightness of the Phoenix Egg. No doubt he would wax philosophical about it.

But it also occurred to her that maybe the reason he did not want her to meet his other form was that was how he carried the Phoenix Egg in and out of the ether.

When a Shifter like Dahlia transformed from her human body into her rabbit alter, her clothes went with the human form and returned with it.

If Aaresh's alter was carrying the Phoenix Egg in his pocket in his other form, that could be how he had been hiding it from her this entire time. He kept referring to his other form as some terrible predator more dangerous than a Lion. And normally one did not think of a predator as wearing clothes with pockets. But since the Lion himself wore clothes, why not his other form as well?

Her only chance, then, was to risk meeting this terrible predator and hoping that she could take the egg away.

Perhaps she was a lunatic. Moon mad. To think she could defeat him in his other form if she couldn't defeat him as a Lion. But then again, maybe *he* was mistaken. Everyone assumed bigger was better; if his other animal was even bigger than his current one, he might assume that meant more powerful, but it might actually make him vulnerable to Dahlia picking his pocket in her rabbit form.

It all came down to one thing. She could not yet give up on her primary mission: Save the earth from a bomb as powerful as a nova.

She smiled at him with false sweetness. "I'm not trapped in here with you. You're trapped in here with me."

The peculiar clock in the center of the room was designed to chime exactly at sunset and dawn every day. It began to chime at 7:03.

Aaresh stepped away from the grand piano. "It's happening now. You better run."

She didn't run yet but she did tense up and position her body and her magic to bolt.

Right on cue, the body of the Lion began to change.

And he turned into the gorgeous, savage, buck-naked

Wild Man.

That's when everything clicked together. The Savage that Aaresh had rescued her from was his other form.

No wonder he had known where to find her.

Furthermore, she should have recognized him. For a moment right after he shifted, the Savage stood very still, and she was able to look at him to study him. His hair was a mess and fell over his face, hiding his eyes and the shape of his chiseled jaw, but now that she was aware of the connection, she could clearly see the school teacher's face and body. Aaresh's Centaur visage was a more refined and civilized version of the Wild Man.

Aaresh Raj had shown her his real face from the start, but she had been too blind to see it.

The Wild Man sniffed the air and his eyes shot to her. Murder, not lust, boiled there. The anger that the Gentleman Lion had shown was only a shadow of the blazing fire of fury that the Savage displayed. Rage that had no ounce of humanity filled his human features and he leapt over the piano and ran at her. She remembered the way he had brutalized the wolves, and she shifted into bunny form, pulling her invisibility spell back into place.

Unlike the last two times the Wild Man had hunted her, she could smell the predation. He was still a wild man, animated by pure fury, But unlike their first meeting in the woods, when his mind had been that of an innocent animal, enough of his human sense of a man aggrieved and betrayed leaked through into this form. It should have been a good sign that his animal and human forms altars were more in tune, but for her it only increased her danger.

He was like the Nietzschean golden beast, a hybrid creature, bristling with complex human resentments and old grudges, yet unleashed from any restraining moral framework or conscience. He had been hurt and now he would kill, the way an animal in a trap would bite at whoever came near it, regardless of the logic or the justification.

He had only his human body, though that body had been honed and trained into a living weapon.

Dahlia drew her crossbow from the ether, and she went on the offensive.

He came toward her, and she shot him. Even as she released the arrow, he began to shine, rapidly, intensely. She realized with dread that in this form, he shared the same magical attributes he exhibited in his Sun Lion form. He was shining so fiercely when the arrow came close to him, it caught fire and burned to a crisp before it even touched him. She shot more arrows but the same thing happened. As long as he could burn up any of her arrows, she could not take him down with the crossbow.

And so she did the only thing that she could. She ran.

And the perfect golden specimen of hyper masculine human perfection chased after her. His body was a work of art, but his lips curled in an ugly snarl and his eyes burned with irrationality. He was both sexy as the night itself and strangely unappealing, because the beautiful mind she had seen during the day had disappeared. He was only an empty shell of himself, beautiful on the outside but devoid of a soul.

Aaresh had said the Wild Man was the most dangerous predator on earth. But Aaresh had sold himself short. For it was not through the body, no matter how handsome she found that body, thathad propelled humans of the Mundane Sphere (and Elves and other humanoids in their own Spheres) to the top of the food chain.

It was the mind, not the body, that was the ultimate weapon.

And right now, for all his strength and rage and magic, Aaresh had disarmed himself.

Dahlia, on the other hand, was still armed with her wits. So although she ran in both her rabbit and her human form, alternating, as he chased her, all was not as it appeared.

I am the huntress, Aaresh, she told him silently. I am the one who will catch you and tame you. You just don't know it yet.

How does a tiny boned fragile woman catch a man who is stronger and heavier and angrier than she? She runs and runs until she catches him.

And that is what she did. She ran in her rabbit form first, because she was faster and more agile in her animal form. She darted underneath the bookshelves. He smashed them to the floor to reach her. She darted around statues. He lifted them into the air and tossed them to get at her. He was trashing the beautiful museum that his other self had collected so painstakingly, and that infuriated her even more than the fact he was trying to kill her. A trapped animal trying to lash out at the one who had hurt him was something she could understand, but watching him destroy the things he himself most valued but refused to recognize in this form filled her with sadness that turned into anger.

I'm not going to let you do this anymore, she vowed. I'm not going to let you keep sabotaging yourself. I'm not going to let you live a half-life. If you want to kill me, you're going to have to kill me as a whole person.

She switched to human form. A weird noise like a roar, but torn from a human throat, a yodel of triumph, reverberated from him. He thought he had her now. She was slower in this form, and she couldn't hide behind shelves or statues.

Twenty-Two

DAHLIA RACED THROUGH THE HOUSE, up a set of stairs, and into the bedroom. She dashed behind the kitchenette counter, grabbing a knife as she went. A leap and a roll carried her across the room, where she planted the knife. There was only one door to the bedroom. She tried to reach it before he entered, but the Wild Man threw open the door and confronted her. She sprinted back the way she had come, across the large room.

With his swifter legs and longer stride, he quickly bore down on her.

Just as he was about to reach her, in the spot she had carefully chosen, she pretended to stumble.

Another cry of triumph erupted from the Wild Man, and then he pounced on her.

As he leapt toward her, seeking to smother her body with his own and dig his teeth into her throat, the way an animal would, Dahlia thrust out her hand, extruding a rope of Water magic just at the level where it hit his shins and tripped him. He fell onto the kitchen knife she had positioned just so. The blade was not there to kill him, but to injure him and slow him down, and it worked as she planned. The serrated edge of the blade slashed into his calf. He roared again, this time in pain.

Such a petty wound would not have stopped him, but all she needed was that few seconds of distraction.

She pulled her Water Rope from the ether and wrapped it around him. The Water Rope was infinite. She usually used it to climb into the sky as far as she needed to get away from someone, but now she used it to wrap around his body over and over.

His fiery heat kept burning the rope into steam, so that it could not get any hold on him, but she just kept spinning more and more. He snapped at the loops of water. He made a face when he tasted it.

He was distracted enough by fighting the rope that she was able to scramble out from under him. She kept the rope coming, loop after loop after loop. She reached deeper into the leylines than she ever had, and she felt the net of magic extend and connect to waters all around the Earth.

He growled and even tried to roar, although in his human form it came out more like a scream of rage.

"That's right, wild guy!" She shouted. "It's saltwater. Do you know why? Because I am drawing from the Pacific Ocean! And every ocean on this planet is connected so I have plenty more where that came from. And if I run out of water on Earth, I will keep reaching deeper into the other realms, and I will pull the Elemental Water out of their oceans too! I will use every ocean in the multiverse to make this rope so you can keep burning it away into steam, but I have more where that came from!"

The Water Rope wrapped around and around him. Even though inside the cocoon of water he was still burning and boiling the water away, she was wrapping the rope so fast that she created a bubble of strands of water orbiting around him. It was almost like the shield around the villa. The shield within a shield. She was still trapped inside with him, but now he was trapped inside the bubble she created, away from her.

She tightened the rope around his neck.

His growling stopped. He met her eyes. Although there was still no civilization there, with his barbarian, wordless cunning, he still understood that she could kill him.

"I could snap your neck," she said out loud.

His gold eyes tracked her, luminosity eclipsed by a shadow of fear.

She didn't want to kill him. But mercy might cost her too much. She was exhausted and unlike his ability to shine, which seemed to go on forever, she *did* feel the weight of trying to pull that much water. The heaviness of it, the gravity, was weighing her down. She didn't know how much longer she could keep pulling on the water rope to imprison him.

Deep within her, a wordless voice wept at the idea of losing him. Her Bunny had not taken anything he'd done as an affront, as Dahlia had. Her Bunny didn't care that he had tried to chase her down.

Her Bunny *wanted* him to catch her. Her Bunny wanted to surrender... and thereby conquer him.

But now... now that Dahlia had the power to kill her enemy—*now* her Bunny screamed inside, desperate and despairing.

I won't kill him! she promised Bunny. Deep inside, he's still Aaresh.

Killing such a magnificent artist, man or lion, would be like robbing the cosmos of a co-creator, like eclipsing the sun, like destroying an irreplaceable work of art.

But what else could she do? He was tiring, but so was she. Sooner or later, he would burst out of her bindings.

And he wasn't only a danger to her, he was a danger to himself. He continued to thrash in the bonds. The wound, from the knife in the trap she had set, blood gushed with each of his furious motions. It wasn't a huge cut, but if she didn't stop the bleeding, he might drain himself. Normally a Shifter would have healed quickly from such a wound, but he wasn't allowing himself even an hour of rest to let his body heal. His furious thrashing, kept re-opening the wound, and kept pumping the blood quickly throughout his body and therefore out the gash in his calf.

Water magic included healing magic. It was not her specialty, Not like invisibility and the water rope. But she had learned enough healing magic to do battle medicine and first aid. She could help the leg wound seal over. It wouldn't be completely healed, but it would stop bleeding and stop ripping open every time he moved.

"Let me heal you," she said out loud.

Of course he only snarled back at her, unable or unwilling to understand her spoken words.

She tried to touch his leg and he gnashed his teeth, nearly reaching her neck. She jerked back again. Even though he was tied up, she couldn't get close enough to him to heal his leg without endangering herself.

She needed to distract him once again.

Right now, he was intent on killing her. But once he had wanted something very different from her. He still had the mind of a simple animal. Could she direct him into another mood?

She put her hands behind her back under her T-shirt and unfastened her bra. Without removing her shirt, she wiggled her arms out of her room and tossed to the side.

"Hey!" She shouted. "Look at me!"

His golden eyes snapped to her. She lifted her T-shirt and undeleted her body, wiggling her breasts.

"Look! Boobies!" she chirped cheerfully.

The transformation that washed over him was almost as dramatic as if he had shifted to another form. She could smell instantly when his entire focus shifted from destroying her to desiring her. And if there had been any doubt, his nakedness revealed exactly where his attention flowed the instant he saw her naked breasts.

She pulled her shirt down again.

He growled at her.

She couldn't help but chuckle. She waved a finger at him. "You only get to see the boobies if you behave yourself!"

Although she had lowered her shirt, his attention and his pheromones remained lustful rather than murderous. She had successfully shifted his attention from one goal to the other. But would he allow her close enough to help heal his leg?

Moving slowly, she once again inched into his personal space. His whole body, and specifically a certain part of him, was stiff and rigid with interest. But this time he did not gnash his teeth at her. He did lean forward, dart out his tongue and caressed her cheekbone. She held very still. He was so close to her neck that if he had tried to rip out her throat, she couldn't have saved herself. But his interest now was different. He traced little hot breathy kisses along her jaw and at the back of her neck.

Her whole body tingled in response. Her inner Bunny also switched moods, from running for her life from him to a sudden interest in getting closer to him.

Oh no you don't! Dang it, this wasn't supposed to work

both ways. Dahlia reminded herself that he was mindless and not at all attractive. But her Bunny wasn't listening. Bunny was thinking about all the ways that wild animal sex might just be the best sex ever.

Not that you have anything to compare it to, she reminded Bunny sternly.

Who cares? Why settle for second-best when you can have the best and never look back?

But you can't have him, Dahlia pointed out. The Wild Man might want to mount her, but Aaresh, the soul of the man, hated her. That thought doused her lust with cold water and she forced herself to focus on the injury. She passed her hands over the gash in his leg. He growled a little, registering his pain, but this time he didn't stop her. And when she massaged the wound with the knitting powers of water healing magic, he made a new sound, a surprised grunt. And a new light sparkled in his eyes. Appreciation.

It was the first time she had seen a more complex emotion in his human face, something other than simple curiosity, murderous rage or naked lust. He recognized that she had healed him, and he was grateful and surprised.

That seemed like a more truly human emotion, not a simple animal reaction, but something more complicated and layered. Was it possible that he was starting to integrate his higher functions with his human form?

She had an idea, a way to test him and find out, but after all the trouble she had gone through to trap him, it was dangerous. It was a risk she was loath to take. But the alternative would be to fight to keep him bound with her water up all night. Although she had told him she could empty out the seven seas of the Mundane Sphere, and all the oceans of the Spheres beyond that, she knew she would tire before she could do any such thing.

And besides. She didn't want to trap him. She wanted to free him.

Was he ready for freedom? Or would he only use his chance to hurt her?

There was only one way to find out. She had to set him free and see what he would do.

Slowly, cautiously, maintaining eye contact with him, she loosened the rope of Elemental Water and drew it back.

The yards in yards of magic spun liquid-silk fell away from him. Even as she watched, the whole bubble seemed to sway and shift, like waves on a shore.

Then, like a bubble on the sea, the whole fragile edifice popped.

He surged to his feet and stood that way, poised. Once again, she was caught by how gorgeous he was, the primeval connection she felt. He drew her to him like the sun drew planets into orbit, and she was helpless to resist the lure. And yet when his eyes burned into hers, full of desire, shyness washed over her; the intensity was too much. Dahlia's lashes fluttered down, while, unconsciously, she wrung her hands. With that burning stare, that pure masculine appreciation for her body, he reduced it to a stuttering school girl, and she couldn't face it.

And he took advantage of her moment of shyness to leap forward, knock her to the ground and pin her body underneath his.

A bolt of fear ran ragged down her spine. "You bastard!" she shouted.

He grabbed her T-shirt and ripped it, simply ripped the entire thing in twain, a demonstration of strength, dominance, and intent. She squirmed, trying to get away, but he pinned her arms over her head, and then he dragged his gaze over her exposed breasts. A supremely pleased leer curled his mouth. He licked his lips, and suddenly all she could think about was his tongue licking her bare skin.

He did lean over her, his tongue darting out, but this time he did not lick or kiss her or even touch her. He let her feel the heat of his breath against her mouth. Her lips parted, opening to the kiss she expected, but contact didn't come. He pulled back and then suddenly stood up and backed away from her. He was still wearing a supremely cocky smile. His whole glorious nude body glowed. It wasn't the same intensity of the shine before that had destroyed her water rope. This was another much more subtle form of Elemental Fire magic. He radiated sheer Charisma.

She moaned. He wasn't touching her anymore but when he stood there in front of her glowing with sex and dominance, her Bunny might as well have been a moth flying toward a flame. Every rational thought flew out of Dahlia's head until she was as mindless with lust as he was. Bunny completely took over and she knew only one thing.

She wanted him. She wanted him now. She wanted him to take her, pound her, claim her. She wanted to completely surrender to him, because she knew there could be no other man for her after this. She would never be able to look at another man and desire him, not after Aaresh had looked at her like that. He hadn't even made love to her yet, but it didn't matter, she belonged to him completely.

He smiled again, both taunting and inviting her, daring her and challenging her. There were no words, but this dance was older than any language, and it was a poetry they both understood by sheer instinct.

He stepped backward once again. He was a cat playing with his prey. He had caught her but released her, because he wanted her to run so he could catch her again.

Desperate to have him close again, she tore off the rest of her clothes. She stood before him as naked as he stood before her.

Then she, too, stepped back. The golden light in his eyes ignited. He recognized the challenge, but he still didn't move forward yet.

He wanted to be coy? She would show him coy. Although she was in human form, her Bunny was as much in charge of her body as his animal was in charge of his human form. They weren't two sensible people in a dispute over some mystical weapon. They were a male and a female in heat. He was determined to have her, and she was equally determined to have him. But she wasn't going to let him take her easily...

Because that wouldn't be as much fun.

She turned around, taking another step, and threw a sloe-eyed glance over her shoulder that taunted him, *Come and get me.*

His eyes, which had fallen to ogle her bare ass when she'd turned around, lifted again to meet her coquettish look. And then finally he leaped forward. She ran, darting out of his reach. But this time when he caught her, as she crawled over the bed, she giggled in delight and triumph.

She now lay on her back in the center of the king-sized bed, while he kneeled across her hips. She had him right where she wanted him. She spread herself under him, and let him look, and reveled in the craving that painted his face when he stared down at her.

Was there any reason she shouldn't enjoy the hot stamp of his lips against her bare flesh, the delightful sensation of his mouth closing around her nipple? Was there any reason she shouldn't rain kisses back on his gorgeous muscular chest or rub her hips up against his hardness?

Who cared? Reason evaporated. She needed him. She needed this. She wanted him inside her.

Then, while they were both lost in the delight of exploring each other's bodies, lost in a paradise of pure carnality, suddenly an annoying sound rang out.

It was the grandfather clock announcing the arrival of dawn.

Her sexy lover blinked at her with a moment of clarity and horror before he staggered off of the bed and transformed back into a giant lion.

Dalia, completely out of her mind with unquenched lust, could do nothing to stop the interruption of her pleasure except scream in frustration.

Twenty-Three

September 23
Sunrise: 07:35
Sunset: 19:52
Moon: New Moon -1
Daylight: 12:04 hours

BY THE LIGHT, *what have I done?*

Aaresh saw Dahlia naked, hair tousled, thrown across the bed like a doll, and his heart broke as well. As much as he had told himself he wanted the Savage to do what he could not bring himself to do, he'd never expected this. He knew now how wrong he had been. He didn't know exactly what the Savage had done to her, but he could tell she'd put up a fight. There were broken and damaged things all over the room, water damage to the carpet, mingled with a pool of blood.

He couldn't bear knowing that Dahlia had spent her

last night of life running in fear, suffering unknown tortures and terrors...

Because of me, he thought, because I can't control my other self.

He reached her side in one leap. Her face, like the entire floor of the room, was drenched in water. He licked her cheek gently. He tasted salt.

The water damage in the room was from saltwater? He sniffed the carpet and realized it was true. It smelled briny, like the sea. He knew she used Elemental water magic, but most Water mages used the closest water source, drawing water either from the air, or since it was very dry here in Colorado, from the rivers and the lakes nearby. Some water mages could even draw on snow, or ice particles in the clouds far above.

All of those were sources of freshwater, though. He had never heard a Water Mage who could draw on the ocean so far from any beach.

Her appearance was deceptive in so many ways. She was much more powerful than she appeared. Indeed, much more powerful than he had given her credit for... Because she was still alive. Somehow, she had survived the night with his savage self. He sniffed her again, and surprise rippled through him. Suddenly he knew why his other self had not killed her, but in a way, it was even worse than what he had expected.

In his Lion form, he found her fascinating, frustrating, intriguing and challenging. He found her physically beautiful, like a work of art, and cute, like a kitten or a pet. But he didn't feel any physical attraction to her. He didn't desire her.

In his human form, obviously, it was a different story. He smelled sex on her body, the sweat from his human self.

He recoiled in disgust at what he must have done. If she had despised and hated him before, how much worse would it be now? Perhaps the best thing he could do was let her put him down like a rabid beast.

She met his eyes; then shame flushed her cheeks, confirming all his worst fears. She covered her face with her hands, rolling away so she didn't have to see him.

By the Light, how she must hate him. He wanted to tell her that nothing was her fault, she wasn't the one who should feel shame, he was. But how could he even begin to apologize? How could anything he said not make it worse?

Still facing away from him, she said, muffled, "I'm too tired to fight you, Aaresh."

"I'm so sorry," he whispered. Of course, since his voice was so loud and rumbly it came out more like the sound of a vacuum cleaner turning on than a whisper. "I'm so sorry for what he did to you."

"What he *tried* to do." She set up and suddenly glared at Aaresh. She slapped his face across the muzzle. He jerked back his head in surprise. "What YOU tried to do. Don't try to deny what you felt and what you wanted!"

"I don't deny it," he grumbled as softly as his vocal cords would allow. "I accept responsibility. I don't even know what I did to you, but it must've been..." He couldn't even continue. He cleared his throat, though it sounded more like a small roar. "I still won't surrender myself to the enemy that would make me use my powers for evil, but I accept the consequences of what I did. If you wish to execute me, give me a clean death, and I will let you. I won't be a slave, but I will die for what I did to you."

That startled her enough that she finally sat up and faced him.

~

Dahlia had never seen a lion look ashamed.

He thinks he raped me, she realized. And he's a good man, so he can't bear it.

She knew she owed him the truth. But then she would have to admit that she had lost control herself, that she had completely surrendered to her Bunny, spreading her legs and thrusting her hips, kissing him all over, as eager for the mindless rut as his Savage self. And that was just so darn embarrassing. She was supposed to be above all that, to be the cool, indifferent huntress, not a lust-crazed fan-girl drooling and wetting her panties over a superstar. If she admitted what she had done, she would have to confess that in his other form, he had a power of her that she had no way to resist, that she had surrendered everything to him—and enjoyed it.

If she could have, she would have preferred to take the easy road, and pretended nothing sexual had happened between them at all. But they were both Shifters, and they could both smell the pheromones in the air.

"Nothing happened, Aaresh," Dahlia said firmly. "Not what you're thinking. There was a tussle, but as you can see, I survived just fine."

Maybe he would let her retain her dignity, and leave it at that.

No such luck. His leonine face crimped with anger and self-loathing.

"No one has ever been able to stop him from doing what he wanted."

"Well, I stopped him."

"How?"

"Ask him yourself. I'm not going to give you any hints

on how to fight me. You're already strong enough as it is."
Her eyes narrowed. "If I fall asleep, are you going to
hurt me?"

He shook his head.

"Good." She yawned. "Because I told you, I'm too tired
to fight you. You were right about me needing sleep..."

She curled up on the bed and fell asleep.

~

September 23
Sunrise: 07:35
Sunset: 19:52
Moon: New Moon -1
Daylight: 12:04

Dahlia woke up in the super king-sized bed. Rays of light
streamed into the room from the French windows and the
sunroof over the gym equipment in the middle of the
room. She could see that it was still just a little after high
noon.

She wondered what she could wear. She had used up all
the clothes she had stored in the ether. She would have to
wear some of Aaresh's clothes, unless she wanted to walk
around naked.

She searched a bureau near the bed and found human
sized clothes in the top two drawers and lion sized clothes in
the bottom two drawers. At first, she wondered why he had
human sized clothes at all, but then she realized these were
the Centaur's shirts, vest, sweaters and blazers, the outfits
she had seen in the glamour. Although the glamour was just

an illusion, if you used real clothes as an inspiration for reference, the illusion was stronger and harder to break. Apparently, that is what he had done. The clothes were still in their packages, or wearing their tags, so obviously they had never been worn in real life.

Also, since as a Centaur, he did not wear pants, the drawers contained only a collection of various tops. She picked out a simple t-shirt and put it on. Even though it was meant for his human form, on her, it almost reached her knees. She took one of his ties and used it as a belt. Now it looked like she was wearing a Roman tunic, like a prisoner about to be thrown to the lions in one of those old classic sandals-and-spears Epic Bible movies from the 1950s.

It felt appropriate.

She left the bedroom and spotted Aaresh downstairs in the middle of the courtyard, swimming in the pool. He was doggy paddling, or, she supposed it should be called lion paddling. He climbed out as she watched and shook the water from his fur like a dog after a bath. Then he looked up and noticed her on the balcony.

His muscles bunched and he leapt to the balcony in a single bound. She made it a little cry and jumped back out of his way. The thump of his landing made the balcony shake. She watched him warily.

"I'm not going to harm you, Dahlia. You know I would prefer to let you go."

"Same here. Just give me the Phoenix Egg, and we can end this game with no one getting hurt."

He shook his head. His mane tossed with the motion, a mass of dark tendrils that looked so soft she wanted to pet him. "It doesn't exist. What your masters want is to own me again. I will never allow that. As much as I don't wish to hurt you, I will kill you and myself before I go back to them.”

“The people who sent me after the Phoenix Egg would not have lied to me.”

He snorted. “You’re wrong. Or you’re lying too.”

“Or maybe *you’re* lying,” she countered. “Maybe you know exactly where the Phoenix Egg is. And maybe you were the one still helping the people who tortured you as a child because your real loyalty is still with them.”

His jaws yawned like a huge cave and he roared so loudly that the sound hit her like a blast of wind and knocked her off her feet.

“Never again dare accuse me of helping them!” he snarled.

She held up her hand in a mollifying gesture, bouncing back to her feet.

“Maybe it’s all a misunderstanding,” she said. “Maybe the Phoenix Egg is among your art collection, and you just don’t recognize it for what it is. Maybe you have it without knowing you have it. Have you thought of that?”

“You had plenty of time to search my house. Twice,” he sneered. “You even had time to set a magical trap to catch me and imprison me on my own property. In all that time did you find what you were looking for?”

“No.”

“Because it doesn’t exist. The only thing in this house that those people value, the only thing they regard as their property that they would do anything to get back? It’s me. They think of me as their masterpiece. If you knew how much money and time they invested giving me the skills and powers that I possess, you would understand why they want me back. To them, I am a weapon, not a sentient being, but a tool to be used. I am what they want, Dahlia. And I will NOT BE the tool of evil!"

She was going to say something more, but just at that moment her tummy grumbled very loudly. A blush painted her cheeks.

"I don't suppose you have anything to eat?"

It would be ironic if what finally killed both of them was not the other but starvation.

He gestured with his head toward the wet bar. "There is the kitchen. There is also some extra food stuff stored in the rooms under the house. You can make and eat anything you like. I've already eaten."

"Let me guess. An omelet made with powdered eggs."

"Yes. I like eggs." After a moment he cocked his head to the side and added roughly, "Also it's the only thing I know how to cook."

The Lion lay in the middle of the large bedroom watching her cook.

"Do you have to stare at me while I cook?" she asked. "It makes me nervous."

"It made me nervous when you stared at me while I played the piano, but you did it anyway."

"That made you nervous? I couldn't tell."

"You can't read my expression because I have the face of an animal."

"On the contrary," she said dryly. "Your animal face is extremely, almost disturbingly expressive."

He growled deep in his throat.

"Why don't you have a kitchen?" she asked. She had found

the storerooms under the house that he referred to. Some of the hidden doors that she had seen when his Shine illuminated them led down into cellars which were packed as well as a FEMA station, rows upon rows of freeze-dried food contained in large storage cans. She found everything she wanted there, except the range of utensils she was used to cooking with. But she did find basics, enough to make a decent meal.

"You *are* in the kitchen."

"This isn't a kitchen. It's a wet bar with a sink and a mini fridge. This house must've had a kitchen when you first bought it."

The golden shoulders of his forepaws rippled in what might've been a lion shrug. "Maybe, but otherwise, the house was much as you see it now. The owner was almost as eccentric as I am. She lives in India, but she has nine houses in nine different parts of the world. This was one of them. It took me a long time to track her down and when I did, she was surprised I was able to find her. She's some kind of fae, I think, but I don't know what. She asked me to play the piano for her and after she heard me, she said that I could buy the house. She told me she would only sell it to someone who could appreciate all the arts. Apparently, she thought I could."

"You play beautifully. I don't know how you do that just using the tips of your claws. For that matter I don't know how to play like that even using fingers. If you don't mind my asking..."

"I mind everything about you being here," he interrupted.

She ignored that. "How is it that you learn to play the piano if you grew up in a laboratory as a lab rat?"

For a few minutes nothing came from him except a low

growl. She assumed he wasn't going to answer her question but then he started speaking.

"It was part of the experiment, of course. Most of the Shifters in the laboratory were treated like animals. Many of them were captured as adults, and were fully human in their human form, yet they, too, were treated as if they were nothing but beasts. However, a few of us were brought to the laboratory as children. Our training was different. It was more like... School. In my case, they wanted to see if they could create a Shifter whose power was not limited by the phases of the moon. They wanted me to be able to change shape right away, without having to learn control over a slow process of trial-and-error like most Shifters.

"Of course, as you have seen, they failed. My powers were never tied to the cycles of the moon, they were tied to the cycles of the sun. By failing to understand that, all they did was switch when I naturally became human and when an animal. And instead of making it easier for me to control what form I shifted into, or to retain my human intelligence in any form, they made it impossible for me to think like a man when I was in the form of a man. They taught me dozens of subjects. Not only the arts that you see in my collection, music, poetry, literature, and history, but science and mathematics. And once I was educated and knew how to get around the blocks they put on the computer, I found the Internet and I was able to teach myself many things they never wanted me to learn. Psychology, for instance. I learned that what they were doing to me was abuse. I learned techniques of prayer and meditation to fight the evil they sought to instill in me. I plotted my freedom and what I would do with it once I had it. That is how I was able to establish the life you see now... the life you want to rip away from me."

"That's not what I want," she said softly. "I don't want to harm you."

Destroying him would be like destroying the Mona Lisa or the statue of David by Michelangelo. He himself was a work of art as well as an amazing artist. Taking him out of this world would be a crime and a tragedy. She remembered the way her body responded to his human form and flushed. It wasn't just his artistic side she appreciated, she had to admit. His carnal side was just as important to her, although she would never admit that to him.

"Why did reversing your daily cycle take away your ability to control your other form?" she asked, hiding her blush by turning back to the pan.

"I don't know."

"I think I know," she said. "You said you studied psychology. Have you studied the psychology of shifters?

"Of course," he said disdainfully.

"Then you know that for most shifters, the animal is tried to our raw, most primitive instincts."

"Isn't that only true for predators? What instinct does a rabbit shifter like you have to resist?"

"Believe me, plenty. For instance..." She trailed off, her cheeks heating again. "It's difficult to say out loud."

A deep, unhappy growl rumbled in his throat. "I think I can guess. It's your flight instinct. I frightened you last night. Dahlia... whatever the Savage did... I mean, whatever I did... I'm sorry."

"Nothing happened between you and me. Okay, I take that back. For the first half of the night, the Savage tried to kill me. I stopped him. For the second half of the night, he wanted something else, but we never... We didn't have sex, Aaresh."

Aaresh looked torn between relief and remorse. "But he tried."

"You don't get it." She sighed, blushing deeper red. But she decided to go ahead and tell him the truth. *Tell him how attractive he is as a man*, Bunny commanded. Dahlia couldn't make herself that vulnerable. Not when she knew that Aaresh would tell her it meant nothing to him, that the Savage didn't care about her as a person, only as an available female.

Yet she owed him some explanation, so she skirted closer to the truth. "If my inner Bunny had her way, she'd hop into bed with every cute guy she met."

She had never seen a lion drop its jaw in surprise. It was pretty funny looking, and she had to laugh. She covered her mouth with her hand to suppress her burst of nervous giggling.

"Does that surprise you? My bunny is a horny little beast who has this alarm going off at the back of her head all the time yelling, 'life is short, enjoy it now before you die.' It's like what you were talking about with the lightness of being. You don't get much lighter than a bunny. Life passes quickly for a rabbit. It's full of uncertainty. But it can be full of pleasure too, and my bunny wants to see it, taste it, and enjoy it. She wants to enjoy the strawberries. I am the one who has to rein her in and control her and remind her that random sex with strangers is not going to bring long-term happiness to the human half of me."

"Ah..." He lidded his eyes and gave her a curious, inscrutable look. "Have you tested that theory? I have to admit I've always wondered what it would be like..."

"Yeah, I bet you have," she said sarcastically.

He flinched. "You don't understand. I am a virgin."

She was shocked. "Okay, I admit I did not see that

coming. I suppose that in the lab... You didn't want to... Or they didn't let you..."

"They tried to force me to breed," he said flatly.

Now she flinched. "That's terrible."

"They couldn't do it. But you have to understand, mindless rutting is the only kind I would ever be able to indulge in. When I am *me*, with the mind of an intelligent person, the only female I could possibly mate with would be a beast, and I would never touch an animal. I would not even want to procreate with a Lioness Shifter in her beast form, because everything in me recoils from the idea.

"But in my human form, I am a true beast, mindless and animalistic. The Savage is not capable of any kind of relationship. It wants to rut the same way it wants to eat. Just to scratch an itch. That's not what I want. But there is no other possibility for me, no possibility of long-term happiness, no true soulmate bond."

She flinched again. That was exactly what she feared. When she lay in Aaresh's arms last night, surrendering herself, body and soul, it meant everything to her. But it meant nothing to him. She gave herself as a complete woman. He was there only in the flesh, not the spirit.

"An ordinary Shifter who has no self-control, is still only cursed to become an animal three nights out of the month," Aaresh continued bitterly. "But I become one every day the sun goes down. And now you know why I am afraid of the dark. It is not the darkness outside that worries me. It is my own darkness that rules my nights."

Twenty-Four

September 23
Sunrise: 07:35
Sunset: 19:52
Moon: New Moon -1
Daylight: 12:04 hours

DAHLIA SERVED him lunch at the tables outside where they could sit together. She could sit in the chair, and he had to lie down next to the table, which put his shoulders just above the tabletop. He ate with his paws. He couldn't truly use a fork and knife, but he used his claws in the same way to slice and poke the food so that he looked incredibly civilized as he ate. It reminded her of the theory she was developing about why he couldn't control his other half. She had started to tell him but had gotten derailed by the conversation about virginity.

When he bit into the omelet, his eyes widened. "How

did you make the food taste like this? You use the same ingredients I do, but when you make the dish, it seems like a work of art."

Dahlia winced. "Yeah, I can cook. I can sew. I can do a lot of girly things. I know what you're going to say. Why didn't I become something soft and sweet, like a pastry chef, instead of a bounty hunter?"

"That's not even close to what I was going to say," said Aeresh, wrinkling his furry nose, "But now that you mention it, why do you want to have such a harsh career when you have so many other talents? Why do you hide your soft side?"

"I hate feeling like a cliché. Oooo, look, a Bunny Shifter who likes to cook, dress up, flirt. A helpless damsel in distress... screw that. I want people to see me as a strong, fearless, kickass go-getter who gives zero fudgesicles about anything."

"And you are all that, but it's not all you are."

"It's different for you. You're a top predator. You have to suppress the wild side of your nature to keep from biting people's heads off. I have to suppress the side of my nature that tells me to run away from everyone—except if I can hop into bed instead. It's not a healthy lifestyle either."

"You're so afraid that if you show your soft side, people will see you as nothing *but* soft, that you've hidden that side of yourself completely. But, Dahlia, it's okay to be a whole person."

"Coming from you, that's rich."

The lion acknowledged this with a wry twist of his fuzzy nose. Aaresh licked the last omelet off his plate. "That was delicious."

"How is it that with everything else you know, you never learned to cook?"

"They never saw any need to teach me that. I got all my food from the cafeteria."

"I suppose the cafeteria also used powdered eggs." She shuddered. They truly were barbarians.

"Now that you are getting to know me," he said, "Do you still think that I would serve the people who turned me into this monster? Do you still think the Phoenix Egg is real?"

"It was the Guardians who told me that it was real. Your sister is a Guardian. Did you know that?"

"I know that she has been forced to work with a group of humans. It doesn't make me trust that group."

"Didn't they help you escape the laboratory?"

He was silent for a moment. "It could've been a trick because they wanted me to work for them. Even in the laboratory, many of the humans were at odds with one another. They argued over which days of the week they would get to do experiments on me.

"There was one team of scientists, the Shifter Research Group, who wanted me in order to find a way to completely control my shifting abilities. They were cruel in one way.

"But there was another group that wanted to turn me into the ultimate assassin. It was actually that group that first pushed for me to learn how to read and write and play music because they wanted me to be as versatile as possible to pass as an assassin.

"It was only when I developed the ability to do those in my lion form that the Shifter Research Group became interested in that ability and allowed me to continue my studies. All of them experimented on me and all of them used me as a tool, but in different ways. The Guardians are just one more such group of untrustworthy humans."

"Most of them are not human."

"But some of them are. The fact that they would work with humans shows they can't be trusted."

"Humans really are the enemy to you, aren't they? But you *are* human. And all the arts and music and literature that you love come from that human half, Aaresh. Lions are noble and magnificent animals, but they don't write sonnets or sonatas. I think that your other self is not as much of an animal as you think. I think, on the country, he also remembers being tortured."

"I don't remember the exact tortures," corrected Aaresh. "I only know that they did it. I have trained myself only to remember the good things. Otherwise..."

"Otherwise, you would act like the Savage, trapped in mindless rage. That's exactly what I think happened," said Dahlia softly. "He is the rock, the primal instinct of self-preservation that you needed in order to survive. You've reversed what normal Shifters do, but you aren't as different as you think. And if you have that in common with the rest of us, then you can control both halves of yourself as well."

"You're deluding yourself because you don't want to give up your mission," scoffed Aaresh. "The night is coming again. You defied the Savage once, but how long do you think you will be able to escape him? You are appealing to *me* to control him, but I can't.

"I *can't*, Dahlia!" His voice cracked. "He will hurt you, if not tonight, then tomorrow night.... If not tomorrow night, then soon. The Full Moon was a week ago and it is waning every night. Your magic is powerful, but I know it is tied to the moon, like most other Shifters. The further away we get from the Full Moon, the weaker your power will be. And then how will you stop him from taking what he wants from you?"

"*You* will control him, Aaresh. You can do it. You *need* to do it, not just to help me but for your own sake. To be who you were truly meant to be in this world. As long as you can't control him, then the people in the laboratory are still running your life."

He shot her a look of pure despair. "I am powerless."

"Fine. Don't say I didn't warn you. My Bunny isn't going to hold back this time."

"If you have to kill the Savage, perhaps it's for the best."

Dahlia almost spoke to correct him, but she held herself back. He hadn't picked up her earlier hint about her Bunny's weakness. Now he was wrong about something else, and she was careful not to let him know. She knew she couldn't bring herself to kill Aaresh, but she had to retrieve the lethal weapon, and Aaresh still refused to help her. As much as she hated it, they were still enemies. She dared not reveal how much power he held over through the sheer sexual charisma of his alter, nor did she dare reveal her power was waxing, not waning.

While it was true that her powers were tied to the phases of the moon, just like every other Shifter, her magic didn't work quite the way he thought it did. Not every animal in the world was either nocturnal or diurnal. Some animals were crepuscular, meaning they preferred to come out in the early morning and early evening. But even more importantly, Rabbit Shifters had an unusual ability to adjust their schedules to the local predators, so they slept when it was safe and could come out when it was safe, regardless of the time of day.

The significance of this for her as a Shifter was that, though Bunny Shifters *were* triggered by the moon, a determined individual could adjust the trigger. She had worked long and hard to adjust her magic schedule. It was similar to the effort she had made to finesse her Elemental Water power. She had taken a common ability and honed it into something uncommon and unexpected.

Just like Aaresh, her magic was "backwards." It was strongest during the New Moon.

The moon was only visible when it reflected the light of the sun. The moon had no light of its own. But the moon did have gravity of its own; and that gravity was present even when the moon could not be seen. That gravity still tugged on the oceans to make the tides, so her Elemental Water power was not impeded by the moon's seeming "absence," but could even be stronger.

The darkness of the New Moon also helped her spells of concealment. All spells of evasion, deception, and illusion were strongest during the New Moon to begin with, including her cloak of invisibility. While Aaresh was radiant, using his shining corona to destroy her magic, he had never come up against her during the New Moon, when her power might actually be stronger than his.

She might be able to bind the Lion and...

Her thoughts faltered. Do what? Torture him into telling her where the Phoenix Egg was? Did she really think that she could do worse to him than had been done during his life by his own caretakers?

She had no stomach for torture.

So that wouldn't work.

What about trickery? Deception was more her style. She could trick him into thinking that she had already escaped. Since he thought he could detect her spell and he expected her to be weaker, not stronger, during the New Moon, he wouldn't realize she was still in the house but invisible. She could create a glamour to make him think she had run away through some means through a gap in the Fire Shield. Then, he would lower his shield to follow her, and she would escape riding on his own back....

She giggled at the idea but her chuckle choked into a sigh.

"I'm not going to kill you, Aaresh. And no matter how much you want to deny your human half, you are the only one in the house with me at night. I suppose I'll just have to let you ravish me," she concluded lightly.

Aaresh didn't share her amusement. He looked horrified. "No!"

The lion paced to the edge of the pool. He stared at his reflection in the water, at the visage of the immense beast with a dark mane and golden fur.

"Marry me," he said suddenly.

Shock made her jerk back. "What?"

The lion turned to her. "I know it doesn't excuse the dishonor of the Savage, or exonerate him if he hurts you, but at least if you have any offspring, they will be entitled to inherit all that I own after you or the Guardians execute me."

"No one wants to execute you, Aaresh."

"A dog who acquires a taste for flesh must be put down," Aaresh said. "I tried to set up my life so that I kept the Savage away from where he might hurt others, but here you are. He has apparently developed a lust for your flesh, and I am powerless to stop his instinct to claim you."

"But you think marriage is the solution?"

"It's not a solution for you or me, but marriage doesn't exist for the couple, it exists for the children."

Dahlia swallowed and turned away. That bastard. He had undone her. Now all she could think about was having a baby with his brilliant golden eyes, with dark bronze skin and wild black hair, with his father's talent for music, art, writing and science. Whether a son or daughter, Dahlia would teach the child to cook and to hunt... why stop with one? This house was big enough for many children, both sons and daughters...

"And how would we marry?" she asked gently. "Marriage is a vow you make in front of your community. You can't do that if you are hiding yourself from the community. Do you know what my mother would do to me if I married without telling her or inviting her to the ceremony? If you don't want a pastor or priest, you at least need a judge and two witnesses."

"I will give you my vow before the Light," he said, "Orally and in writing."

"No," she said. "I can't marry you if you are suggesting it only out of fear of your night self. I'm not your charity case. I can handle the Savage, and how I do it is none of your business. Unless of course, you take control. I could marry a man with your mind, Aaresh, a Shifter in charge of both his forms. But I can't marry a lion and a Savage."

He hung his head. "Then we are both doomed."

Aaresh couldn't stand to be around her, knowing how she must despise him, and how he deserved it. He padded away on four paws. In the music room, he sat down at the piano and began to play. In his heart, he knew Dahlia was right. He had to take control of his alter form. He couldn't allow the beast to win.

Light, let me control my baser self, he begged. The words

didn't matter as much as the yearning of his soul, which he poured into the music.

I love her, the song told him. *And if I cannot learn to be a man, I will lose her.*

Twenty-Five

September 23
Sunrise: 07:35
Sunset: 19:52
Moon: New Moon -1
Daylight: 12:04 hours

WHEN THE CLOCK chimed to warn the sun was setting, Aaresh was still playing music as he felt himself incandesce from a lion into a man. His mind didn't snap away as it usually did. He remained in control of himself even though he was also aware of all the human emotions he had long suppressed when in his human body.

Would he lose his mind if he stopped playing? He feared he would, yet when the song came to an end, he let his fingers—long, human digits, not paws—come to rest on the ivory and ebony keyes.

Someone drew in a sharp breath. He looked up and saw Dahlia.

He was thunderstruck. Slowly he rose and approached her. She watched him, her expression strange. For the first time, he consciously noticed how gorgeous she was. Not just beautiful, aesthetically speaking, but desirable.

Sexy.

She ducked her head, half-closed her eyes, smiled at him and started walking toward him, stripping off the tunic she wore during the day. He could see her arousal in the way she walked, smell the fragrance of the dark shadow between her legs. Watching the play of light over the taut muscles of her belly and thighs, he was instantly aroused. He was about to tell her that she didn't have to fear his sexual desire anymore because he was still in control, and he would leave her alone tonight. He would spend the night playing piano... he hadn't done so in his human form in a long time...

"Since when are you so shy, you sexy beast?" she asked him. And then she threw her arms around him and started kissing him passionately. She rubbed her body against his.

Shocked and horrified, he shoved her away from him. She staggered backwards, shocked. He had forgotten that he was as strong in this smaller body as in his lion body, thanks to the magical interventions used to alter and deform him growing up.

"What are you doing?" she cried.

"What are *you* doing?" he demanded.

Her jaw dropped. "You can talk!"

"It's me...Aaresh... I tried to do what you told me, to remain in this body. I did it for you, so that I could save you from myself... And then I find that you are... You were going to let him...?!"

"Why not?" she snapped back. "I decided to meet you on your own terms."

"I can't believe you were going to do that!"

"So what if we came together like two adult human animals, not under the influence of any drugs or any form of magic except our own nature, and we did what came naturally? And there's nothing wrong with that! You're the one who told me I shouldn't be afraid of my soft side. I chose to embrace it."

She walked back up to him and poked him in the chest. "You look me in the eye right now and tell me that you don't want me."

"I don't know *what* I want," he said. That wasn't true. Her scent was driving him crazy with desire. He hadn't felt this way since... since the first time his jailors had tried to trick him into mating with someone, and he'd vowed never to surrender to their plans. "I thought... Whatever happened to what you told me about resisting what your bunny wanted? About how you knew it wouldn't lead to your long-term happiness? Suddenly you just throw all that out the window because it is convenient to control me through sex?"

"Control you through sex?" Dahlia snorted. "Maybe... but maybe it's more like sexual healing."

"So you're doing this out of pity."

"Stop trying to twist this around into something bad."

"So... should I let go?" he asked. "Should I let the Savage have this body back? If it's him you want, not the real me..."

"Aaresh! *This* is the real you. The whole you." She traced his masculine jaw. "Don't you think it's interesting that the same night I finally decided to give in to my wild side, you finally found a way to tame your wild side? There's something beautiful going on here. I said that I wouldn't have sex with someone I didn't respect, and I am keeping to that. I'm not going to lie, I find you sexy as hell when you are in this body." She moved her hands over his broad muscular chest and then let her fingers lower toward his thighs. He grabbed her wrist. This was torture. He was torn between desire and reluctance.

She tilted her head up to his face. Even when they were both in human form, he was so much larger than her that the top of her head barely reached his shoulders.

"But I also respect you, Aaresh. Your soul and your spirit. Your courage and your sensitivity. Your ability to see the world in new ways and express it through music and poetry and writing. You are so amazing on so many levels. Terrible people tried to break you into pieces, but even in pieces you're more of a man than anyone else I've ever met. I want all of you, and if I have to take some of you in the morning and some of you at night, I'll take you anyway I can."

"That's not what you came here for," he whispered.

"You're right. That;s not why I came here. It's not what I thought I was looking for. It's what I found. I have a confession to make. My power is tied to the New Moon and it's at its peak right now. I was planning to trick you. I thought I had to in order to save humanity from a terrible weapon. But now that you've crossed the final threshold, I know that you really are in control of yourself, I don't need to do that. I do trust you even if you don't trust me. I'm going to lower my shield now. If you let me, I'll return to the Guardians and tell them that you don't have the Phoenix Egg. I'll tell them that you're a good man." She smiled. "And a good lion."

Even as she spoke, she proved her words by lowering the Water Shield. She could feel the rush of the water which had formed a sphere around the property for so long disperse and evaporate into the atmosphere and the earth.

"I decided the same thing," he whispered, "to let you go even if it means you might turn me over to my enemies."

The fire died down and all that remained were wisps of smoke.

"Then here we are," she said softly. "But it's nighttime, and I don't want to go home in the dark. I don't want to be alone tonight. Will you let me stay with you? Will you make love to me—with all of you?"

"No," he said.

She flinched back.

"Unless," he said, "You promise me this thing between us will outlast the night. Will you still love me tomorrow? Will you marry me?"

She glowed. "Yes."

He bent his head and kissed her.

～

September 24
Sunrise: 07:35
Sunset: 19:52
Moon: True New Moon
Daylight: 12:01 hours

Aaresh woke up in bed next to the most beautiful woman in the seven spheres. *I'm the luckiest lion in the world.* But he wasn't a lion right now. He was still a man and he was gloriously naked and satiated. He stretched out on the big bed, watching her sleep next to him. He wanted to wake up every morning exactly like this for the rest of his life.

Out of habit, he did check to see if the shields were still

in place. He reached out with his mind and felt at the magic, probed the edge of his property. The Water Shield was still gone. The Fire Shield was also down.

For the first time he wondered if she was telling the truth about the Phoenix Egg. He certainly had not taken anything like that on purpose. And he didn't see how he could've stolen something by accident. But he had been so busy trying to convince her that she was wrong, he never stopped to consider if *he* might be wrong.

"About this Phoenix Egg... What made you so convinced that I have it?"

She cracked open an eye. "It's not even sunrise yet and do you want to have this conversation?"

"I don't know if I'm going to turn into a lion at dawn or not." He stroked the hair from her cheek and brushed it back behind her ear. "I want to enjoy every moment I have with you. I know it can't last."

"Why can't it last, Aaresh? Why can't we make this a permanent thing?"

"When you report back to your masters, they are going to send people to capture me and lock me in a cage somewhere and I'll never see you again."

"You can't still believe that."

"I do."

She sat up. "But you lowered the Fire Shield!"

"Yes." He smiled sadly. "For you. For a night with you, I am willing to live in a cage again for the rest of my life. As long as you are alive and free. My only fear is that they lied to you as well, and that after you report back to them that you don't have the gizmo they covet, they will turn on you and put you in a cage too." His face contorted, his human face. "I couldn't stand that, Dahlia. If I could give you what you wanted, I would do it."

"I don't understand it," she said. "According to the compass you *must* be holding it. How could you *not know* if you are holding it?"

"You never showed me how this compass works. Maybe it's broken."

"I'll show you now."

Twenty-Six

September 24
Sunrise: 07:35
Sunset: 19:52
Moon: True New Moon
Daylight: 12:01 hours

AARESH STOOD in the center of the room, and she pulled the crossbow out of the ether. He switched to his Lion form, whether in response to the threat of the weapon or because he could no longer resist the morning sun pouring through the skylight, she did not know.

"I'm not going to hurt you, but the compass is attached to the crossbow. I aim it by pointing the arrow. You can see why I didn't try to show you how this worked before. If you still don't want me to aim a crossbow at you, I can see if I can detach the compass..."

"Just show me how it works," he growled, his lion voice deep and scary even though he wasn't trying to frighten her.

"If you were going to betray me, I actually prefer you kill me yourself then turn me over to them."

There was no need to explain whom he meant by 'them.'

"I'm not going to kill you, Aaresh. The compass is set to find the Phoenix Egg. Now watch what happens when I face away from you. I'll face due North first."

She turned her back on him and faced the other direction. She lifted the compass. Although she didn't move, the bow turned her around on the pivot of her heels until she faced Aaresh.

"Now I'll try to face south." She walked around him and again put her back to him with the bowand the arrow pointing to the south. Once again, the magical crossbow turned her back around to aim the arrow directly at him. She did the same routine with the east and the west, facing away from him and letting the compass magically twirl her around. No matter what direction she went, the crossbow compass moved to point the crossbow directly at him.

"I told you so," he said. "There is no Phoenix Egg. I am the target."

She sighed. "I don't believe the Guardians lied to me. But maybe somebody lied to them. Maybe you're right. In that case my mission is over. There's nothing to search for." She paused. "But what if I'm wrong? What if there *is* a Phoenix Egg, a Doomsday Weapon, with all the power of an egg-sized nuclear bomb, and I'm just not looking for it in the right place?"

"All this talk of eggs is making me hungry for breakfast. I don't suppose you would make one of your delicious thank you bunches, would you?" He smiled. "I would love an omelet."

"All right," she said. "Let's break for breakfast."

Suddenly she wiggled her eyebrows. "Maybe that's what you did with the Phoenix Egg. Maybe you ate it. Have you ever actually made an omelet with fresh eggs?"

"Once or twice. Sometimes they kept eggs in the refrigerator at the lab and I would sneak in and cook them in the office kitchen before anyone could catch me. One time I found a huge…"

He broke off. He made a strangled noise Like a cat whose tail had just been stepped on. "What did you say? Maybe I… ate it?"

"Oh no. Please tell me you're kidding."

"That's not possible, is it? Even if I had eaten it, that would destroy it. You wouldn't still be detecting it with your magic bow and arrow?"

"I don't think it would be that easy to destroy. It's a magical item. But how could you eat the egg of a phoenix and not know it?"

"When I was a child, there was another prisoner with me who was a phoenix. He was a father figure to me as well as a mentor. Our captors allowed the relationship because he was one of my tutors. They fed him Phoenix Eggs, which I thought was odd, but he assured me that unfertilized eggs contain nutrients for chicks. It's not cannibalism, it's like a baby drinking milk. I knew they were doing experiments on him, including trying to turn him into some sort of weapon, but he was a male. He didn't lay the eggs. As far as I knew he died, and they were unsuccessful.

"I would never eat the fertilized egg of a phoenix, the egg that hatches out of fire and becomes a new sentient Shifter. But what if the egg I found was not fertilized, and was kept refrigerated because it was actually a half mechanical device that had been turned into a weapon? The shell of a phoenix is made out of metal. Very rare metals working together in a beautiful pattern. The egg I ate was like that as well, but I thought nothing of it because it was in the refrigerator. True it was in a special container but..."

"When did this happen?" she asked.

"Shortly before I escaped." He paused. "Shortly before I escaped, I developed the ability to use nuclear combustion magic. Before that I could only use ordinary Elemental Fire. I was working on my magic in secret, trying to find ways to get away from the humans without them stopping me. I thought that I found a way to tap into deeper magic by practice. I never connected it with the omelet I stole when I snuck out of my cage one day, but now that I think about it, I swallowed the egg only a few days before I discovered my new power. That's also when I started to develop a new level of Shine. I had always been able to radiate a halo of light, but it was only then I started to shine so brightly I wasn't able to control it. I had to work hard to hide it from the humans..." He trailed off, aghast at what he had inadvertently done and how close he had come to destroying himself and others.

"I can't believe it," She said. "You ate the egg but it was too powerful to destroy. And you were too powerful to be destroyed by it. Instead, its powers transferred to you... the mutant properties became absorbed into your own magic. You were right all along, Aaresh. You *were* my target from the start, but nobody knew it, not the Guardians who gave me this assignment, not me, not the Azir at the laboratory, and apparently not even you. Nobody realized it because nobody could have conceived of it–that *you have become the Phoenix Egg*."

His lion face expressed unutterable horror. "Does this mean I have become a doomsday weapon?"

Dahlia reflected his dismay back to him. "I don't know."

"I think it does. I think it means that I am a walking bomb."

"We don't know that. Let me take you to the Guardians and they can examine you and..."

"No. I don't trust them. If I am a walking bomb, they may want to threaten others with my existence."

"They wouldn't do that."

"I can't take that chance. And that's what you've been trying to tell me all along, isn't it Dahlia? You are the one who told me how dangerous the Phoenix Egg is. You were the one who convinced me that the macabre laboratory would create such a weapon and be willing to use it. Now I know why you couldn't afford to let me go. You were right all along. Now that I know the truth, I can't afford to let myself fall into the wrong hands. Before, to let you go, I was willing to take the chance that my enemies would capture and cage me again. Now I can't do that. I would be risking your life and the lives of billions of people on this planet."

"Maybe they can find a way to separate the bomb from your body. Please, you must come with me..."

"Tell me what you were going to do with the Phoenix Egg when you thought it was just an ordinary magical device."

"I was supposed to throw it down a deep shaft into the crust of the earth and then use a magical lighter to donate it. Once it was destroyed safely within the earth's mantle, no one could ever use it again."

"Then that is what we must do."

"After we separate the bomb from your body!"

He shook his leonine head and his mane wagged side to side. "No, now that I have guessed the truth, I can sense the power within me. I realize it was originally foreign to me, but it has become fully integrated into my Sun magic. There is no way to separate it, any more than you could separate my skin from my flesh and still leave me alive. The only way to be rid of the bomb is to end my life."

"Aaresh! Don't ask me to give you up when I just found out I love you!" Her eyes burned with tears, but he could tell she knew he was right.

"I thought I could never find my true mate, like a normal Shifter," he said softly. "Then, like a miracle, I found you. Even if we can't be together, I am grateful that I found you, Dahlia. I thought I was beyond being loved and yet you love me. I love you. I would do this for you alone, and I would do this for the world alone, but I love the world more because I know even if I die, it will have you in it."

"No, Aaresh..."

"You know I'm right, you've always known. Our feelings don't change what must be done. In fact, my love for you only makes me more determined. Take me to this mineshaft, I will climb down, and you will detonate the bomb."

Dahlia wept and argued but she could not convince him to change his mind because she knew he was correct. The compass kept pointing at him no matter how she willed it to point away. If the Phoenix Egg was no longer a threat to the earth, the compass would not have kept pointing at it. The Emperor had been specific about that. It was one way she could test if the detonation had worked after she flipped the lighter. As long as the compass kept pointing at Aaresh, he was still a walking bomb, exactly as he had explained.

They both knew what had to be done. It didn't matter if he lost his life, and she lost her heart. There were more lives than their own at stake.

She had argued before that a wedding without witnesses wouldn't be valid, but now she surrendered to exchange personal vows with him, with the Light alone as their witness. Aaresh used magic to heat and flex a titanium paperweight into two matching rings. Then he pulled out his favorite volumes of love poetry to find words, which they chose together. There was so much they wanted to say, and so little time before they had to do what must be done.

"I wish I had time to write an original poem for you," said Aaresh. "I would write that to love another person is to see her fully, and be seen fully by her in turn... without clothes, without shields, without shame... but I don't know how to put the words together yet. I could spend a lifetime trying to find the words. But I don't have a lifetime, do I?"

She had to turn away to hide her tears, but he saw, and knew.

They adapted a poem by Rumi for their vows. They held hands and faced each other:

Dahlia spoke first:

"The moon has become a dancer at this festival of love.
This dance of light, this sacred blessing, this divine love,
beckons us to a world beyond; only lovers can see with their eyes of fiery passion.
They are the chosen ones who have surrendered."

And then she added, "As I have surrendered to you, now and forever..."

"And as I have surrendered to you," said Aaresh. "Now and forever." He continued the poem:

"Once they were particles of light, now they are the radiant sun.
They have left behind the world of deceitful games.
They are the privileged lovers who create a new world
Truly seeing each other
with eyes of passionate light....

"As I see you," he finished. *"Here and hereafter."*
"And I see you," she said. *"Here and hereafter."*
They put the rings on each other's fingers and kissed.

That night, they made love one more time; they shared one last meal. Dahlia made an omelet, adding all of the vegetables and mushrooms and spices that he had somehow forgotten to add. They joked and talked about their favorite movies and then when they could no longer speak because the horror of what had to be done hung over them, they dressed.

They were both in their human form during all of this, and Aaresh remained in control as if he had never had any difficulty. Only the fact he sometimes started to make a movement more suitable to a quadruped, then caught himself and stared at his human hands in surprise, gave away how new this was for him.

He looked at her with the same handsome face as she

had seen before. But now she saw intelligence as well as passion in his golden eyes; infinite sadness as well as love.

"I love you," she said. Her voice broke. "I don't think I can do this."

He took her hand in his. His soft human hand had smooth skin and he stroked her palm as if wondering at the feel of it. ("It feels different than when I touch you with my paw," he had told her when they were making love.) Now he said quietly, "You can do it. And I can do it. Because we must."

Twenty-Seven

September 25
Sunrise: 07:35
Sunset: 19:52
Moon: True New Moon
Daylight: 12:01 hours

AARESH FOLLOWED Dahlia to the entrance of the shaft in the mountain. The location in the wilderness was too close to the laboratory where he had been held a prisoner for many years to make him comfortable.

"No wonder I have never seen it before," he said. "I would never come this close to the base unless I had no choice."

The valve to the underground shaft had been buried under dirt and leaves, so it took both of their Elemental magic to find the exact opening and pry open the metal door. She used her Water magic to wash it clean and he used

Fire magic to burn away the rust on the wheel locking mechanism.

He kissed her one last time. "If I had not been stupid enough to swallow a doomsday weapon, then I would stay with you forever, if you would have me."

"If you tried to leave me for any other reason, I would tie you up with a ribbon of water and make you stay by my side," she said. Tears were streaming down her cheeks. He caught one of her tears on his human finger and brought it to his lips. "You are so tiny, but you have all the power of the oceans in you. You will live a long and happy life even after I am gone."

She shook her head. His expression hardened.

"Promise me that you will so I have the strength to do this, Dahlia. Be like the sea. Don't let the ebbtide carry you away but come back to the shore stronger than ever."

"Then for you I will try," she said but she could barely get the words out over her tears.

Mocking laughter erupted behind them. "Isn't this a touching scene!" sneered a derisive voice.

Aaresh stiffened with his arms around Dahlia.

A tall thin man with a large nose and dark hair strolled out of the woods where he had been watching them, probably concealed by a deception spell much like Dahlia's, linked to the New Moon. His eyes blazed red. It was the Hellhound who had been sniffing around Aaresh's classroom.

Suddenly he shifted into his Hellhound form, which was canine in shape but as large as a pony. Unlike a regular dog, his feet were like a vulture's talons. He snorted fire.

Instinctively, Dahlia wrapped both herself and Aaresh in a veil of insensibility. But the Hellhound was used to

Water magic and was still able to run toward their position yapping and barking his jaws.

"Quick," she whispered to Aaresh, "I will distract the hound, you go down."

"I can't do this if I fear you might die as well. I'm doing this to keep you as well as the rest of the world alive!"

"You do what you have to do, and I'll do what I have to do! Go! I can handle one Hellhound!" Dahlia pressed a lighter into his hand. "This is the detonator," she said. "Don't let them win."

Reluctantly, Aaresh nodded and started climbing down.

Aaresh knew Dahlia could handle one Hellhound and that gave him the courage to climb down into the shaft. But just as she was closing the hatch over his head, he heard barking and the arrival of more Shifters. He recognized the smell. It was the pack of White Wolves who had been hunting him.

"We claimed the Bunny Shifter as our kill!" he could hear them saying.

And then he heard the sounds of fighting and realized that he had left the woman he loved to face not just a Hellhound, but an entire pack of White Wolves all on her own. As powerful as her magic was, he had a sick feeling in the pit of her stomach that he had left her to die.

And yet what could he do? He had to destroy himself before either the Hellhound or the White Wolves dragged him back to their own masters. He had a feeling he knew who each group served. The White Wolves were the classic servants of the Winter Elves. It was their job, disguised as ordinary dogs, to help the human teams round up shifters and bring them back to the laboratory to be experimented on.

But there were also darker, more dangerous creatures who had an interest in the laboratory and its results. He knew there was at least one demon who was very interested in the results. He didn't know the demon's name, but he knew that Hellhounds were in the service of Darkpyre.

He used his elemental wind magic to carry him down into the shaft faster than he could climb. He landed at the bottom. He could sense the mass of the earth pressing in on him and knew he was deep into the crust of the planet. This chimney in the Earth was not natural, nor made by any mundane geological process; it was a leyline of Elemental magic, created out of a braided helix of Fire, Stone, Water and Wind magic—all four elements. Usually, leylines consisted of only one Element or another. To create a hub of all four like this must have taken amazing skill and control. Based on the flavor and flair of the magic, Aaresh sensed that the Magician had created this node, but long ago, for it was over a century old. This tremendous weave of power was connected to hundreds of leylines, like the center of a spider's web. This deep into the earth, he could feel the raw magic that grew from the Magician's Castle like roots from a tree. This was the trunk of the leylines of power that the Magician must draw upon when he used magic at the Castle.

He could feel the leylines glowing like hot veins in the rock. Focusing his vision with Elemental Fire, he could glimpse them, like x-rays through the rock. They pulsed and glowed with unearthly light, radiant with magic.

I must die to save the world, he reminded himself. *And yet if I die, Dahlia must fight my enemies on her own. If only I could get rid of the bomb without destroying myself,*

I could climb back up to the surface and fight next to her. I could be with her, and protect her, not only today, but all the days of our lives to come...

He pressed his hand against the leylines and with his other hand he held the lighter. He didn't need it, he realized. Deep inside himself he knew what he had to do to explode. He could tap into all the hatred and all the sorrow and all the grief he had ever felt. He could destroy himself and miles of rock all around him in a cataclysm of self-destruction.

Or... he could shine.

He could be reborn like a phoenix.

He closed his eyes and let the radiance around him increase. He let the weight of his magic implode until every different form of physics from all the Spheres and all the nine kinds of magic fused into one pin prick of light.

And then he ignited with the power of a thousand suns.

The White Wolves showed up in their canine form. They attacked the Hellhound that was about to attack Dahlia. She knew they weren't really trying to defend her. They were only trying to stop the other bounty hunter from getting their prey. But the result was the same. The Hellhound fought the White Wolves, and it was an even match between the four of them and the one of him.

In fact, it began to look as though all by himself he would destroy all of them. He broke the neck of the first Wolf. He set the next one on fire. The last two fought harder than the others, but he finally snapped his jaws around the neck of a third one and bit his head clean off.

Finally, the last remaining White Wolf switched to its human form. It was Zachery.

"You idiot!" shouted Zachery. "While you're wasting your time fighting us the lion is getting away! We both serve the same master, why are you killing us?"

"I told you, dog, I am my own master," snarled the Hellhound. "You are nothing but flea-bitten curs in my way."

The Hellhound leapt at Zachery, but suddenly he was jerked short. Dahlia had unwound her rope of water and wrapped it around him. In the new moon, her power was at its peak. The Hellhound thrashed and tried to break the rope, but she poured all the power of seven seas into the thin thread, and he could not break free.

Zachery looked at her and she saw the conflict in his face.

"Get out of the way," he snarled. "Let me save the life of the lion. He might not like living in slavery but it's better than dying."

Zachery leapt at Dahlia. She couldn't maintain her focus on the lasso and fight him off at the same time. He knocked her over and she felt his jaws close around her throat.

Suddenly a bolt of shining light shot out of the hole in the ground. The White Wolf shrieked in pain, blinded by the light. He whimpered like a puppy and scampered away in the snow trying to escape the heat and brilliance. Dahlia's rope of water melted, thent evaporated into boiling steam. The Hellhound had also been blinded by the light, but instead of running away, the Monster made of smoke and darkness and brimstone, lunged at the light, trying to smother it.

But the light was too strong. The light, she saw now

that her own blindness was receding, was shaped like a lion. The lion and the shadow dog fought fiercely and no mercy was asked or given. Finally, the Lion snapped the neck of the Hellhound. The creature disintegrated into black oily smoke and disappeared.

Aaresh switched to human form and hurried to her side. "Dahlia! Are you okay?"

"I'm alive," she gasped, "but what about you?" She didn't want to berate him for not killing himself but she was terrified that the threat of the detonation still hung over them. She knew he must've returned to help her fight off the hound and the wolves, but she couldn't bear to send him back down in the shaft a second time to die. She just wasn't that strong. She wrapped her arms around him and sobbed. "Don't leave me again."

"I don't have to," he said. "I don't have to leave you. I won't. I'll never leave you." He rained kisses down on her head and she lifted her face to him like a sunflower to the sky.

"But I don't understand. The Phoenix Egg..."

"The Phoenix Egg hatched," he said and he broke into a huge grin. "I am as much Phoenix now as I am a lion. And if you knew how much I loved the Phoenix who taught me so much of what I know, the teacher who taught me right from wrong in a place where there was nothing but evil, you would know how happy I am that I am now a true son of the man I always considered a father. "

"I still don't understand," she said.

"I will tell you everything," he said, "but I hope you were right about the Guardians you trust so much. I hope they are not evil, Dahlia. Because I just gave them a huge infusion of power. I have to meet them now and make sure

I have not made the worst mistake of my life. Will you take me to the Magician's Castle?"

"The Castle? I have never been there. It was the Empress and Emperor who hired me from the dragon mountain..."

"No," he said family. "The Castle is at the center of the leylines. The Castle is now the center of the new energy grid. We must go there and I must meet all of the Guardians, not just the Empress and the Emperor but also the Magician."

"And your sister, "she added. "She is desperate to know that you are safe. I couldn't promise..." She broke off, feeling ashamed that she had ever considered hurting him.

But he kissed her. "I understand. Take me now. I must meet them and find out the truth."

Twenty-Eight

September 25

IN THE END, they both switched forms and she rode on his back because that was the fastest way for them to travel. A bunny riding on the back of a lion would have been an amazing site had any humans been around to see it, but even arcanes were not aware of the two travelers, for Dahlia cloaked them both in invisibility.

When they reached the Magician's Castle, they were met by a Jinn who refused to let them inside. Aaresh crossed his arms and glowered, so Dahlia explained why they were there.

"The Guardians aren't to be disturbed right now," said the Jinn. "If the Empress hired you, I suggest you go to her mountain and await her. When she's available, she'll see you."

"We must speak to the Magician himself," said Aaresh.

Neither man would budge, so the argument continued

until a cheerful blonde woman in a sky blue cardigan skipped down the corridor to meet them. The pert blonde introduced herself as Bethany Guiscard.

"Are you Moxie's brother?" Bethany asked Aaresh directly.

He nodded. Suspicion radiated from him.

Bethany, however, acted breezy. "It's fine, JZ," she told the Jinn. "We've been looking for Moxie's brother forever! I'm sure everyone will want to see him. I'll take him up."

"What about the woman?" demanded JZ.

"Dahlia is my wife," said Aaresh flatly. "I won't go without her."

"You're married?" Bethany's eyes bugged.

Dahlia and Aaresh nodded. Dahlia worried that the Guardians might be upset and chide her for being unprofessional. A bounty generally wasn't supposed to marry her mark.

But Bethany clapped her hands together. "How wonderful! I love that you didn't waste any time. May I touch you both? Just a precaution. We've been betrayed recently, and it stings."

"She's a Null," Dahlia warned Aaresh. But when Dahlia held her hand out to Bethany, Aaresh did the same, though his eyes narrowed to golden slits, as if he expected Bethany might try some nasty trick.

Bethany clasped each of their hands in turn. It didn't hurt. It felt no different than shaking hands with a mundane human. Even Aaresh couldn't complain.

Bethany apparently learned something more from the touch than they did.

"Oh my," said Bethany. "I think I see what's happened. Everyone was so focused on finding the Tower and the Star, because they were sure they had found the pattern of the

Call of the Light. But I said, 'Be careful...sometimes life is more messy than the patterns we try to shove it into,' you know what I mean? Just because something happened one way yesterday, doesn't mean it *has* to happen exactly the same way today. What's the saying? 'History doesn't repeat, it only rhymes.' Am I right?"

However, she didn't wait for a reply, but bounced away down the corridor, forcing them to follow her or be left behind. She led them through elegant hallways and then up the spiral steps of a tower.

"What did you mean, the Guardians have recently been betrayed?" asked Dahlia.

"Ah, it's a sad story," said Bethany. "Prince Vanemor of the Azir Elves came to us and claimed to have received the Call to become Guardian of the Tower. He also claimed he needed to defect in order to claim his true love. He fooled us all, then he sabotaged some very important spells my husband had prepared in case of conflict with the Azir and their allies. Then Vanemor and his Goblin accomplice absconded with the blueprints to the Castle. Alephander was furious. It's not often someone plays *him* for a fool."

"That's terrible," said Dahlia, although privately she wondered if Bethany should be revealing this information to relative strangers. It wasn't wise to advertise the weaknesses of the Guardians.

"Yeah, it sucks," Bethany prattled on, "Not only because, oops, important stuff was destroyed and other important stuff was stolen, but we thought we'd found two more Guardians, but haven't. And Alephander says that we can't afford to get behind. If we're attacked before we have all the Guardians, some 'prophecy' says we'll lose." Bethany made a face and air quotes when she said *prophecy*.

They reached the top of the tower and entered a round

stone room lined with knick-knacks. At the far end of the room stood a large bank safe. Bethany walked up to it, casually opened it and swung open the door.

A tunnel of rainbow light swirled inside the safe.

"It's a Gate!" exclaimed Dahlia.

"What Sphere does it connect to?" demanded Aaresh.

"If you want to speak to the Guardians, you'll have to follow me," said Bethany. She grinned at them, as if she knew the punchline to some joke they did not. "Let's see if you can. I suggest you hold hands."

Bethany entered the tunnel of light. Dahlia and Aaresh exchanged a glance, made their decision, held hands and followed her. It was odd walking in the tunnel of light, which swirled around them as if they were walking through a coruscating nebula in the star-spangled cosmos, yet their pathway was as firm as if walking on solid ground.

At the end of the tunnel, they followed Bethany through another door, emerging into a classic basilica sweetened by rays of golden light that poured through a stained glass dome and other high windows.

Seventeen Guardians sat at a round table right under the luminous dome. The Magician, Alephander Guiscard, was the only one standing, and he immediately noticed Bethany, and the fact that she brought two guests with her.

The other Guardians were all seated at the table, arguing with each other.

"And what can we do now?" demanded Victoria. "We have no way to stop them short of open war!"

"We must avoid war in Mundania," said another man, whom Dahlia recognized as Pastor Mike. "That would lead to millions of deaths. If the doomsday weapon is detonated, that number could be billions of deaths!"

"You don't have to worry about the doomsday weapon!" Dahlia said loudly. "Aaresh has disposed of it."

All of the other Guardians turned and stared in astonishment at her and Aaresh.

Aaresh switched into his other form. Why, Dahlia didn't know. But she had to admit that the shining lion the size of an elephant made an impressive sight.

The Magician looked at the lion who was gently glowing like a lightbulb. "Do you have something to do with the sudden infusion of energy into the leylines underneath Arcana Glen?"

Aaresh was about to answer when suddenly a small kitten ran from the group of twenty people and leapt onto the lion's mane. The kitten turned into a girl with cat ears. She had tan skin and brightly colored hair but she was obviously related to Aaresh. He switched back to his human form.

"Moxie!" he said. "It's me. I go by Aaresh Raj now."

"You can speak in your human form!" she exclaimed. She hugged him again. "I have been so worried about you! Why did you run away after you were free?"

"You can catch up with your sister later," said the Magician. "Explain the burst of energy we detected. It had the strength of a doomsday weapon and yet the town seems to be stronger rather than weaker."

"Because any energy that can be used to destroy can also be used to create," said Aaresh, "Just as fire can be used to burn or to cook, or nuclear energy can be used to bomb or to light up an an entire town. That is my gift to Arcana Glen. It is a reactor, embedded deep within the crust of the earth, that will provide both mundane and magical energy for centuries to come. It works on the same principle as the sun and as the other magical elements that come from the different spheres that were merged in the Phoenix Egg. But now these energies have been harnessed for the powers of creation and sustenance, We provide light and heat to everyone, rather than for destruction and an endless winter."

The Magician narrowed his eyes thoughtfully. Then he looked at Dahlia. "And what was your role in all of this?"

"I could not have done it without her," said Aaresh.

The Emperor and Empress both stepped forward and explained their role in hiring her to find the lion and the Phoenix Egg. Many other discussions and exclamations broke out among the Guardians, but Dahlia only cared about the fact that her hand was clasped in his. They were both in human form, although the light still glowed around him when he forgot to dim it.

"Come," said Emperor Troy, "Accept your thrones and join us at the table."

"W.. what?" stammered Dahlia.

Moxie punched her brother in the arm. "Don't you get it? You both entered the Temple of the Guardians. You could not have done so unless you both are Guardians." She scratched her chin. "I have to admit, I'm a little weirded out that you're the Guardian of the Tower..."

"Aaresh Raj is the Guardian of the Sun," said Alephander. "And Dahlia Moon is the Guardian of the Moon. We have not yet located the true Guardians of the Tower and the Star."

The Emperor looked at them gravely. "You can accept or refuse the position of Guardian. We cannot force you to do what you reject. But please be aware that time is of the essence. We are fighting a war, and although the Mundane Sphere is supposed to be neutral, the enemy does not respect that. We have taken away their most dangerous threat, the doomsday weapon. But they are still building the tower. You've heard of the Tower of Babel, haven't you? It was a tower that was built to connect all of the different spheres magically together into one giant stairway that the demons wanted to use to storm the Three Immortal Spheres, the Last Home itself. Now they are building another one."

"I don't wish to seem ungrateful," said Alephander sardonically, "But your gift is a double-edged sword. Yes, you've increased the power of the leylines for the Castle and the town, but you've also created a ready source of energy for their tower."

Dahlia gasped. "That was not our intention."

"It could not be helped," said Alephander. "But combined with their other victories recently, they are advancing their conquest and we are on the defensive once again. They deliberately surrendered Autumndelle to convince us that Vanemor was the true Guardian of the Tower. They would not have accepted such a loss if they did not intend to extend the war to Mundania. If they capture Mundania, they can easily re-invade Autumndelle on two fronts."

Dahlia remembered how strong the Hellhound was. He was just a servant of the demons, less powerful than them as the White Wolves were less powerful than the Winter Elves. How strong would an entire army of demons be?

"What can we do to help?" asked Aaresh.

"Join us," the Emperor said simply. "Join us and join the fight."

Dahlia reached her hand under the table and took his and squeezed it. Their eyes met. He tilted his head and she nodded. She knew they shared the same thought.

"We will help you," said Dahlia.

"Yes," agreed Aaresh. He made the single word into an iron promise.

They would not need a month or a year to decide what they needed to do. They both knew what their decision would be. But they would not be fighting alone. They would have the other Guardians beside them. Warmth radiated from his hand to hers, and she was aware that, subconsciously, he emitted a gentle glow. She felt that warmth and light deep inside her, reflecting the love she felt and knew that whatever challenges they faced, they would have each other.

If you enjoyed this book...

Please write a review on the site where you bought it. Even a line or two helps indie authors like me continue to bring you more novels to enjoy.

You can also write to me if you would like to tell me which character in this novella you would like to know more about! Several characters who appeared here are certain they will never fall in love, but the Light may have other plans.... Whose story would you love to read?!

If you liked this book, you will also enjoy the other novels and novellas set in Arcana Glen. These are all stand-alone Happily-Ever-After romances set in the Arcana universe, with recurring characters and an ongoing alternate history. Each series has an interconnected overarching story, but still has its own Heroine and Hero and happy, complete ending. Each book, even within a series, can be read and enjoyed independently.

Next up in the Major Arcana series is **_The Moon Bunny & the Sun Lion._** As with all the Arcana Glen romances, this is a complete love story, but related to the ongoing quest to find all the new Guardians and the murderer who framed the Magician for the Massacre of the old Guardians.

Also check out the holiday novellas in the same universe. These shorter holiday-themed novellas in the Arcana Glen Cycle of the Year series can be read any time of year, just like any Arcana Glen novels.

Be sure and grab **_The Genie & the Gymnast_**, a stand-alone Prequel sweet paranormal romance to The Major Arcana series.

The Unfinished Song (Epic Fantasy):

- Initiate
- Taboo
- Sacrifice
- Root
- Wing
- Blood
- Mask
- Mirror
- Maze (September 2022)
- Sworn (Coming)
- Flute (Coming)
- Wheel (Final Book - Coming)

Arcana Glen Sweet Paranormal Romance Novels:

- The Magician & the Fool
- The Seeress & the Seraph
- The Dragon & the Slayer
- The Witch & the Warrior
- Moxie & the Maverick
- The Lawyer & the Leprechaun
- Death & the Detective
- The Demon & the Dryad
- The Moon Bunny & the Sun Lion
- The Tower & the Star
- Judgment & the World

- The Tree & the Egg

Arcana Glen Sweet Paranormal Holiday Novellas:

- The Genie & the Gymnast (available only here)
- The Tarot Reader's New Year Promise
- The Griffin's Fake Valentine Bride
- The Leprechaun's St Patrick Day Heist
- The Prodigal Wolf's Second Chance Easter Romance
- The Mermaid's Spring Fling Romance
- The Shifter's Best Friend at Beach Wedding
- The Sheriff's Magic Summer Jail Break

Science Fiction:

- Conmergence (short story collection)
- STRAT (Military Science Fiction)
- CIVIS (Strat Book 2 - Coming)

Books on Writing:

- 30 Day Novel: No Fail Formulas to Finish Your Novel

Kavio is the most powerful warrior-dancer in Faearth, but when he is exiled from the tribehold for a crime he didn't commit, he decides to shed his old life. If roving cannibals and hexers don't kill him first, this is his chance to escape the shadow of his father's wars and his mother's curse. But when he rescues a young Initiate girl, he finds himself drawn into as deadly a plot as any he left behind. He must decide whether to walk away or fight for her... assuming she would even accept the help of an exile.

~

"I was enchanted by Initiate, drawn into a world that felt as comfortably recognizable and uniquely untried as Narnia, Hogwarts or Middle Earth."

CASEE MARIE, THE GIRL WHO
STOLE THE EIFFEL TOWER

"Wow. Holy smoking wow. This is one of the few books I've read that I can honestly say was totally, 100% original.... However, as unique as it is, it was insanely easy to slip into the story..."

EMI LONDON, OCTOPUS INK

"I recommend this [series] ...to fantasy and epic saga lovers and readers who liked reading Lord of the Rings, but found the length of the book overwhelming....This book series has a unique concept - breaking down the traditionally long Epic Fantasy tale into shorter more manageable books."

GINA, MY PRECIOUS: RAMBLINGS OF A KINDLE ADDICT

Start reading Initiate right now!

I WENT OUTSIDE.

No doubt about it, Neraka ain't the nicest planet in the universe. It's ornery. Even those of us who love it and wouldn't consider livin nowhere else won't say otherwise. But Neraka got its own kind of beauty.

The air was clear and the wind was putterin about real mellow like. Accordin to my kit, the temp was a balmy −20 C, warm enough to melt the SO_2 snow into sloshy tarns, but not so warm that the glaciers had started steamin.

I took the footpath up to the top of the canyon, and then around Cutter's Ledge to the Tarn of Hidden Castle. Ain't no castle there that I ever seen. The tarn is just a regular mountain lake, pretty enough, sure, but nothin special. The liquid sulfur dioxide was shinnin just like it was molten gold, and the reflection of the pink gas giant, Heaven's Rose, danced on the ripples of the lake. The krakenweed-covered rocks, half submerged in and about the lake, looked like ladies trailin their long locks into the water. Below, I could see twinklin lights from the spires and spikes of houses down in the canyon. The houses themselves were underground, so all that showed were the uplink spires, elevator shacks, and guntowers.

Sure can't blame the Sulphines for building their castle here, if they ever did. Nobody reports havin seen them in years and years, and some folks reckon they packed up and left on account of the human traffic on the road gettin more and more. Time was, Tarn Croft was the end of the line, but that ain't been true for close on a century now. So it seems, them Sulphines was right to be worried that we humans would outbreed them, but they couldn't fight us no more, so they just moved on. And thinkin on that, and lookin out at the lake of gold, it made me kinda sad somehow.

I took the torch and walked as close to the edge of the lake as I dared. One end of the torch was pointy, and I dug that into the edge of the lake. The other end of the torch was wrapped in a fine wool of shredded steel and magnesium. With a tool built into the gauntlet of my kit, I ignited the steel wool. It burned fitfully in the sulfur dioxide air. Then I stepped back, acause I knew what was goin to happen and I didn't want no sludge on my boots.

Sulphine plants use sunlight to make sulfur trioxide, and the Sulphine animals and people react the sulfur trioxide with sulfur to give sulfur dioxide again. The most common "plant" is krakenweed. We call it that acause it wiggles like tentacles. It ain't much more than stringy colonies of single celled plants and single celled animals in symbiosis. The plant cells take in the light and the ciliated animal cells give it the wiggle. Krakenweed falls dormant during the local-night, but the plant cells ain't particular about their source of light, and burning a flame can wake them up.

Sure enough, little tentacles of slime started to squirm out of the lake toward the light.

Wakin the krakenweed is supposed to bring the Sulphines out, them sulfur breathin natives of Neraka that's people-shaped and people-smart. I waited, kinda breathless, kinda half expectin them to appear. I went outside.

No doubt about it, Neraka ain't the nicest planet in the universe. It's ornery. Even those of us who love it and wouldn't consider livin nowhere else won't say otherwise. But Neraka got its own kind of beauty.

The air was clear and the wind was putterin about real mellow like. Accordin to my kit, the temp was a balmy -20 C, warm enough to melt the SO_2 snow into sloshy tarns, but not so warm that the glaciers had started steamin.

I took the footpath up to the top of the canyon, and then around Cutter's Ledge to the Tarn of Hidden Castle. Ain't no castle there that I ever seen. The tarn is just a regular mountain lake, pretty enough, sure, but nothin special. The liquid sulfur dioxide was shinnin just like it was molten gold, and the reflection of the pink gas giant, Heaven's Rose, danced on the ripples of the lake. The kraken-weed-covered rocks, half submerged in and about the lake, looked like ladies trailin their long locks into the water. Below, I could see twinklin lights from the spires and spikes of houses down in the canyon. The houses themselves were underground, so all that showed were the uplink spires, elevator shacks, and guntowers.

Sure can't blame the Sulphines for building their castle here, if they ever did. Nobody reports havin seen them in years and years, and some folks reckon they packed up and left on account of the human traffic on the road gettin more and more. Time was, Tarn Croft was the end of the line, but that ain't been true for close on a century now. So it seems, them Sulphines was right to be worried that we humans would outbreed them, but they couldn't fight us no more, so they just moved on. And thinkin on that, and lookin out at the lake of gold, it made me kinda sad somehow.

I took the torch and walked as close to the edge of the lake as I dared. One end of the torch was pointy, and I dug that into the edge of the lake. The other end of the torch was wrapped in a fine wool of shredded steel and magnesium. With a tool built into the gauntlet of my kit, I ignited the steel wool. It burned fitfully in the sulfur dioxide air. Then I stepped back, acause I knew what was goin to happen and I didn't want no sludge on my boots.

Sulphine plants use sunlight to make sulfur trioxide, and the Sulphine animals and people react the sulfur trioxide with sulfur to give sulfur dioxide again. The most common "plant" is krakenweed. We call it that acause it wiggles like tentacles. It ain't much more than stringy colonies of single celled plants and single celled animals in symbiosis. The plant cells take in the light and the ciliated animal cells give it the wiggle. Krakenweed falls dormant during the local-night, but the plant cells ain't particular about their source of light, and burning a flame can wake them up.

Sure enough, little tentacles of slime started to squirm out of the lake toward the light.

Wakin the krakenweed is supposed to bring the Sulphines out, them sulfur breathin natives of Neraka that's people-shaped and people-smart. I waited, kinda breathless, kinda half expectin them to appear.

I was halfway back around Cutter's Edge when my kit started wailin at me that it had detected somethin. For a wild minute, my heart started in thumpin, and I thought maybe them Sulphines was goin to show themselves after all. Didn't take me no more than a wink to realize what a fool notion that was. We ain't never found a good way for our sensors to pick up sulfur-based life at any distance, acause their heat and composition signatures blend too well with their environment. Only somethin metal, somethin silicon, or somethin human, would trigger my kit's alarm like that. My sonar and thermal was both blinkin at me like mad.

I powered up my armor to full amp. No longer a dead weight of near a hundred kilos, now it would amplify my movements if I needed to move real fast or real strong.

Tarn Croft got a bunch of outlyin sensor mines in the canyon, plus the two big watchtowers. I radioed them all, patchin my kit in to eyeball their pickup in my visual field. My corneal screen flipped from one pickup to another, but none of them showed anything, not on sonar, not on thermal, not on lindar. A chill took a crawl right down my spine. That meant whatever was creepin towards Tarn Croft was doin it real sneaky like, and it knew just how to avoid all our towers and sensor mines.

Slow, though. At least, there was that. And, whatever it was—*whoever* it was— hadn't reckoned on *me* bein out here. That was a bit of luck for our side.

The sheriff and his boys was all at my weddin, but he always keeps an eye on the view from the lighthouses through his kit. He must have sensed it when I patched into them, and he buzzed me now.

"Charlie?" he asked, audio only. "You okay, boy?"

"I think there's somethin out here, sir," I buzzed back. "Somethin big, somethin smart. Can't be a passenger car so far from the road, but there's enough heat that there's gotta be at least one man in one vehicle, maybe more."

"Shit." The sheriff was silent a minute, maybe shocked, or maybe talking to somebody else on another link. After a minute: "Charlie?"

"Yessir."

"I'm goin to round up a posse. Meanwhile, you're the closest. I hate to ask you on your weddin night, but..."

"You can count on me, sheriff," I said quickly.

"Now, boy, I don't want you gettin into no trouble," he lectured me. "Ain't worth the pain I'll get from your ma if I let you kill your fool self."

"I'll just get close enough to get a visual on it for your boys, sheriff, I promise. You reckon it's oxy rustlers?"

"I don't reckon nothin just yet. We better maintain radio silence from here on out, but if you get into cold sulfur, you better holler, you hear?"

"Yessir. Charlie out."

Click here to keep reading STRAT.

THE HOT DOG DETECTIVE

BETRAYED BY HIS WIFE, *mocked by the man who murdered her, fired from the police department, MacFarland remakes himself as a hot dog vendor. But then a murder draws him back into the justice business...*

Betrayed by his wife and the system, former Denver Police Detective Mark MacFarland dropped out of the system...all the way. But now he has put drinking and homelessness behind him, bought a hot dog stand, and started a new life.

Then a noted defense lawyer asks MacFarland to prove that his client was wrongly accused of murdering her husband. Suddenly, MacFarland's past catches up with him.

. . .

Aided by his former partner, Cynthia Pierson, and his longtime homeless friend, Vietnam Vet Rufus, MacFarland discovers the husband's murder is actually part of a larger web of conspiracy...and may even tie in to the death of his wife.

Read the first book in this cozy mystery series with a slow burn romance for free.

Click here to read.